SANCTIFIED

The Spirit & the Flesh are Contrary

FREAK

SANCTIFIED

The Spirit & the Flesh are Contrary

FREAK

B.Y.SMITH WRITES

For more information & books by B.Y.Smith Writes,
visit www.bysmithwrites.com

Dedicated to my Daddy
Mr. Ernest Edward Smith
Your legacy lives on.
Love,
Your Baby Girl

Acknowledgements

MY MOMMY:
Edna Mae Smith

MY CHILDREN:
Andrea S. Campbell
Devonte' M. R. Tillman
Jurnee A. Tillman
Iyana S. Tillman
She'Kera Brooks (Also book cover model)

Brendan Edward Campbell (For letting GG stay up late)

Victoria Adams
Viandra Pryce
Ram Seetharam
Exodus Design Studios
Tracie Lynette Baldwin

Last but not least:
My Spiritual Father, Pastor James F. McCormick III,
for always pushing me to be all that
God has called me to be.

This is only the beginning
of what God wants me to do.

Table of Contents

CHAPTER ONE

Stressing

All my life I have been in somebody's church. When I was a little girl, Mama and Daddy said, "As long as you live in our house, you are going to church." Sound familiar to anyone? My brother Lamar and I heard that phrase our entire childhood and our parents meant it. We lived in Winterville, Florida and my parents did not believe in leaving us home alone. So this is how our week went. Sundays were reserved for Sunday school at 9:00 a.m., morning worship at 10:00 a.m., 5:00 p.m. for BU and I don't even remember what that stood for, and 6:00 p.m. was evening worship. Mondays mama had deaconess meetings and we had to go along. Tuesdays mama had choir rehearsal and we were there as well. Wednesday everywhere was mid-week service and I guess this was so people could stay saved until Sunday came again. Thursday was kids' choir practice, which was my favorite. Lamar did not like singing in the choir so he always tried to get out of practice. However, he was okay once he got there because he enjoyed playing the drums. Friday nights Daddy had deacon meetings, so if mama wasn't home, we were at his meeting with him.

They made us get up to pray and read a daily scripture as a family, and say our prayers before bed. I promised my parents when I became grown that I was never going to church—*and I meant it*, until I became an adult and real life struggles hit me in the face, I fell in love with Edward, and things just got crazy. Edward was a little taller than six feet, weighed close to 200 pounds, skin dark and smooth, and his big brown eyes talked. Oh, yeah things got crazy! This brother was fine, and I had vowed to save my body for Mr. Right. Edward sho nuff looked right to me. I then realized that I, Tamara Daniels, needed Jesus and He was the only way I could honor my vow to myself.

Edward wanted to elope, so he proposed to me on Valentine's Day in 2007, about six months into our relationship. I loved him and believed he loved me too. Nonetheless, eloping was out of the question. I told him that we were too young, and I wanted to finish college. I told him that once I received my Bachelor of Arts Degree in Business Management, we could get married. He agreed, so we set a wedding date for August 30, 2008. Not only would I be anxious about graduating, I would also be panicky about getting married a month later.

I remember when I started feeling like an adult and feeling stressed about things. It was Monday July 28, 2008 and Edward and I had a huge argument. We had an understanding about us waiting until we were married. Not that I didn't want to break a brother off. He and I had discussed this—*he thought it was great*, but now Edward was getting weak. Neither of us had given our life to Christ at this point, but because of my upbringing, I wanted to wait until marriage. We kissed and hugged, rubbed and snuggled; but with limits. Who was I kidding? After all those verbs, we ended up pretty heated. *NOT SMART!*

I was going to be graduating in two days with my B.A. from the University of North Florida in Jacksonville. Although I was excited that I was finally getting out of school and moving off campus, it had also been two days since our argument, and I had not talked to him or heard from him. Edward graduated three years earlier with a B.A. in Music and now was the Production Coordinator for the well-known Jazz Festival nationally and internationally. It was not uncommon for us to miss two or three days talking on the phone or even by Skype, but he would never let a day go by without sending a text saying, "Love you, babe." I had nothing but bad thoughts fluttering through my mind: What if he misses my graduation? Is he with someone else? Is the wedding still on? I was nervous but I had to stop— Edward had never done anything to make me doubt him, or question his love for me. It's so close to our wedding day, God should understand if we had sex, right? Edward is a good man and had been waiting for me for almost two years. Why didn't I elope when he asked? All he wanted to do was make love to the woman he loves. He is only twenty-five years old, and has done very well for himself. He has a job he loves, makes good money, has great benefits, and travels. He purchased a home in Stone Mountain, GA, and told me numerous times "this is our home." Plus, he found me. Amongst all those nervous thoughts I remembered: Mama always told me "A good wife will be found, you ain't got to run after no man, Proverbs 18:22." She programmed that in my head. What more could a woman want?

I was up all night worrying. I knew I had to shake these thoughts and focus on my graduation. My parents would be here in a few hours and I did not want them to see me this way. With them arriving a few days early, Mom and I could find a dress for the wedding. She claimed there was nothing in Winterville. We just loved to go shopping together. Plus, they could take me out to dinner. Their presence would positively cheer me up. I loved being around my parents. They spoiled me rotten and I was a brat when I was around them. Lamar would be arriving a little later in the evening with my best friend Samantha. They tried to date for a while, but now they were just friends. Samantha broke up with Lamar because he wanted to have a sexual relationship too. I wonder how they got past that? Sammi and I never discussed it. I couldn't just be Edward's friend.

I wanted to be his wife. We were meant to be husband and wife. We were waiting, and grant it we probably shouldn't have put ourselves in a few of the heated situations we were in, but we never went through with it. That was most likely why he was so pissed off right now, from me teasing him. Mom would always say, "Child cover your butt and tits, and stop showing that man all you've got! Why the man gotta buy the cow when the milk is free?" Lesson learned: Cows shouldn't tease men. She would also say, "Don't play with fire and you won't get burned." Mama always had some kind of crazy quote or a scripture to throw at me. I guess if things don't work out for me and Edward, then I most definitely have been BURNED. I had to gain my composure and pretend nothing was wrong, or mama would start quoting, and I was not really in the mood to hear it. However, I honestly should take mama's advice because she and daddy had been married for 40 years and she was a virgin when they got married.

Oh, well, I was eager for mama and daddy to arrive; I had my bags packed to go stay at the Wingate by Wyndham with them. The Wingate was only about a mile away from campus. My parents were timeshare owners and mom used points to book a jacuzzi king suite for her, daddy, Sammi and I. She also booked an executive suite for Lamar and Edward. The reservations were for July 30th, until August 6th so they could help me load up all my stuff to move back to Winterville. Once I got to Winterville, I would be with my parents for three weeks, and then off to Stone Mountain with my new husband only a few days later. I had told Edward that we didn't have to have an expensive honeymoon; I had never been to Stone Mountain, and just going there with him would be good enough for me. He said, "No, I'm taking you to Italy for our honeymoon." How perfect was that? It also was convenient that the 2008 Rimini Jazz Festival, in Rimini, Italy, was September 1st – 5th and his company paid for him to go and covered all of his expenses. Well, I guess him purchasing my ticket wasn't convenient, so I was appreciative and really excited about the whole thing. Nonetheless, we were still going to Stone Mountain first. That was, if he still had plans to marry me.

The more I thought about it, I had not done anything wrong. I was starting to get ticked off now. Who did he think he was? Got me sitting here stressing about his black butt. I didn't even know if he was dead or alive. He didn't even know if I was dead or alive. This was child's play. He knew from the start that I wanted to wait until I was married. He agreed that he could handle it and respected my wishes. How was he going to wait thirty days before our wedding to get mad? What kind of person does that? Wow! This was really blowing me. WHATEVER !!! I went to breakfast.

CHAPTER TWO

Super Freaks

The closer I get to graduation day, the nastier the breakfast on campus tastes. That's so crazy because it hadn't bothered me for the past four years, only the last two weeks. I was homesick. "Hey baby girl," came from behind me and I knew who it was. "Daddy!" I ran and gave him the biggest hug I could. I stood in his embrace, taking in a deep breath smelling his cologne. "I missed you so much daddy." "Hello little girl, remember me?" I looked over and saw mama standing with a purple and teal outfit on; my mom could dress. "Oh mama, you know I missed you too." I missed both my parents, but I was without a doubt a daddy's girl. Mama and I talked openly, but daddy used to take me to work with him on days there was no school. We watched those old corny sitcoms together, and we just had a great bond. Daddy was the reason I wanted to wait to get married before I had sex. He had told me that he was proud that I was still a virgin at eighteen; so I knew if I waited until I was married, he would be pleased. Pleasing my father was very important, and I was not about to let Edward's little fit make me question my beliefs anymore.

7

"Mom you look amazing as always." Mama looked good for her age; she was fifty-nine years old, 148 pounds, kept a cute haircut, and still had a coke bottle figure. Daddy loved the virtuous woman my mama was, and he spoiled her too. He was very proud of his stunning wife and I am pleased to say that the apple didn't fall far from the tree. I made it my business to exercise and keep my body in shape, because I wanted a marriage like my parents. I wanted a man to adore me the way my daddy adored my mama. I'm sure that isn't the only reason he loved ma so much, but it didn't hurt. Watching my parents love one another was very inspiring; no, they weren't perfect and they argued, but I never saw my mama and daddy mad the next day. Nope, once the sun came back up, mama and daddy were smiling and laughing together. I remember them having a table called the "settlement table." I recall going to bed late a few nights and my parents were still sitting at that settlement table after an argument. I always heard mama tell daddy, "We are not going to bed angry with this unsettled. That was our vow from the start; Ephesians 4:26." I guess they had some kind of agreement before marriage. I didn't know, but by morning they were talking again as if nothing happened. However, I do remember going to bed one night and waking up at 4:00 a.m. to go to the bathroom and they were still there. I thought to myself, "They need to get a life," not realizing that they already had a grip on life. They honored God and His Holy Bible, and they obeyed scripture.

Once I became a teen I wanted to know what Ephesians 4:26 said and meant. "Be ye angry, and sin not: let not the sun go down upon your wrath" (ASV). After reading that, I knew I would somehow incorporate that in my marriage one day. I think that is why mama would quote scriptures so much, so Lamar and I would subliminally receive the Word of God without knowing that we were. Nevertheless, mama and daddy were in love. They still went on dates, took walks in the park, and held hands. I asked ma one day, "Ma do you and daddy still have sex?" She looked at me, looked at her body and said, "What do you think? Marriage is honorable among us, and our bed is undefiled. Hebrews 13:4, you just don't be labeled among fornicators and adulterers—because then God will have to judge you." Hearing that let me know that they still got their freak on. My mom was always taking me into Victoria's Secret with her. She would go into the dressing room while I waited and then come out and make her purchase. When I became a teenager, I realized my mama was a sanctified freak. I would never tell her that, but it was kind of funny and gross at the same time. That was another reason I wanted to save myself for marriage. So many of my friends had divorced parents, or cheating parents and I never knew my parents to go through such things. I figured mama and daddy were doing something right, and the biggest thing that was consistent in their lives was God. Although I had vowed when I was younger never to go to church, this dilemma I was going through right now with Edward let me know that I would need God in my marriage, and in my life.

I was so ready to go. I already had my bags with what I would need until Saturday, and the hotel wasn't far away so if I needed something else Sammi and I could go and get it. "What are you eating Baby Girl?" Dad asked. "It's supposed to be oatmeal Daddy, but I'm done and ready to go." Mama noticed I had not eaten any of it. "Why didn't you eat? Are you hungry? Do you want to go and get something?" "No Mama, I just want to go so we can get a massage and I can get in the pool and do some laps." They both looked at each other kind of weird and seemed to be okay with that. I hope they don't think they're fixing to be freaking on my weekend. Old nasty selves…smh. Now how I'm gone pray with these people in the morning? Well their bed is undefiled, but still…I wondered what time my brother and Sammi would be here? I need someone else to chill with, plus I wanted something to get my mind off Edward.

We arrived to our hotel, and it was so beautiful. There was an indoor pool, the grounds were kept up so nice, and although it looked like a normal hotel, their jacuzzi king suites and executive suites were very spacious. After we unloaded our bags Daddy went to park the car, and we walked into the hotel. I reminisced on when we took family vacations when I was a little girl, and I missed Lamar. Our parents took us on vacation each year. The hotels weren't as extravagant at first, but as time went by they got nicer and nicer.

Daddy and Mama used to work for a cleaning agency cleaning buildings, but now were the owners of their own company called Clean Shine Janitorial Products. They provided essentials such as: trash bags, toilet tissue, paper towels, bleach, and other cleaning essentials to over thirty companies. It's been up and running for about twenty-five years now and my parents rarely go into the office. Mama looks over the books and has a meeting with dad once a week about what's going on. Mama and Daddy actually still does the hiring, when it is needed. There is very little turn over in staff because it is a great company to work for and not many employees. Lamar and I worked there when we were teens in the summertime, but now Lamar is the office manager. I may be going back to work there if Edward doesn't…

"Tamara…Tamara," Mom was tapping me. "Ma'am, I'm sorry. I was thinking about Lamar and how we use to play on the elevators at the hotels we would visit on family vacations. Why did y'all let us go out by ourselves and play in the halls at the hotels? You never left us home alone." Mama and Daddy looked at each other and laughed… they're so nasty. They're like super freaks. OMG! Daddy went to check in and Mama turned to me and said, "I hope Lamar hurries and get here so we can send you to play on the elevators," …then she laughs "Ma stop!" She was making me nauseous.

It was only 11:45 a.m., but it seemed as if it was the longest day ever hanging with Mama and Papa Freak. So, I asked, "Can we please go get a massage now?" "Yes we can, baby." So, Mama and I went to get a massage and Daddy went to take a nap. I told Daddy to listen for Lamar and Sammi. He said, "I will. Y'all have fun and if you decide to go shopping without me I won't be mad, I promise." Daddy hated shopping with Mama and me. If he could just go with one of us it wasn't so bad, but going with the both of us was not something he ever wanted to do.

Mom and I walked to the Massage Green Spa located in the Winsor Common Court next to Publix. The spa was very close to the Wingate and we both liked to walk, so that was not a problem. Should I tell her about Edward? I am not surprised that they haven't said one word about him. I am

Mama and Daddy's baby, and although they were okay with us getting married, they didn't want Edward taking me all the way to Stone Mountain, Georgia.

CHAPTER THREE

Spa Time

As we were walking things felt kind of awkward. Then Mama said, "Spill the beans little girl." "What do you mean Mama?" I replied. How does she always know when something is wrong? "You know what I mean; you haven't said one word about that big-headed Edward since we've been here. What's wrong?" She was right on it, I burst into tears. "Oh Mama, I haven't talked to him since Monday. We had an argument." "Calm down baby it's only Wednesday. You know his work is very demanding this time of year. Maybe he's busy." "I know Mama, but even when he is busy, he always sends me a text before I go to bed."

Then she turned into Lecture Mom. "Tamara Monique Daniels...," anytime she called me by my whole name I knew I was going to end up with a headache. "Edward is not your husband yet, and already you are questioning his time." I tried to jump in, "But Ma..." "Listen now. If Edward walked away from you today, you would still survive." Again, I tried to interject, "I know..." "Shut-up, that's your problem. You need to be silent so you can listen." I dare not cut in again, so I quietly listened to Mama speak. "If you are going to trust him, trust him and don't try to analyze every missed phone call, every call answered on the first ring, or every rushed conversation. You say you love him, so just trust and believe that there is a good reason he hasn't called. True love is patient, kind, and not easily angered—1 Corinthians 13:4-7," I knew a scripture was coming. Then she said, "If you truly believe that God sent Edward to find you, trust God and He will work this out for you." I asked her, "So I shouldn't be mad?"

Before Mama could answer, we had arrived at the spa, and the concierge greeted us. "Welcome to Massage Green Spa, my name is Nicole; do you ladies have a scheduled appointment for today?" Mama and I looked at one another dumbfounded. I read the sign on the wall, "No walk ins." and my mouth dropped; but mama composed herself with such elegance and said, "No ma'am we don't have an appointment, but I am sure you don't mind fitting us in, we would like the works." Then she looked around and leaned closer to the woman and said, "Looks like your staff needs a worthy cause for the pay they will be receiving for today." I looked around and there was no one in the building except employees. My mama was a little arrogant at times, but the next thing I heard was Nicole's voice – "Would you ladies like to be in the same suite?" I looked at Mama, "Of course, we would." "Please follow me," Nicole said as she headed towards the massage area of the spa. Then Nicole handed us robes and said, "Here are robes for you ladies to put on. Please knock on the door when you are done and both of your masseuses will be waiting for you." Mama knocked on the door, the two masseuses came in. Once the massage started both Mama and I were quiet, almost asleep because the massage was so relaxing. I knew I was tired from being up all night worrying about Edward, and I guess Mama was too from the ride up.

While I was getting my massage, I thought about what mama said, "You need to be silent, so you can listen." Both of those words have the exact same letters in them. Being silent allows you to hear and clearly understand what's being said. How does she know that I scrutinize when Edward answers the phone too fast or tries to rush me off the phone? My mama amazed me; she really is the best mother ever.

Mama and I didn't discuss Edward again, at least not at the spa. We were too relaxed to talk during our massage, so we enjoyed being pampered and the relaxation that came with it. After the massages, we were ushered by Nicole into the salon area so we could receive our pedicures and manicures. Nicole asked us if we would like a drink, and I asked, "Do you all have any lemonade?" Mama would have a glass of wine only when she had a spa day, so I knew what she was going to say. "I'd like a glass of Verdi if you have it. Any flavor will be fine, but I prefer raspberry." I quickly said, "Oh, I'll have what she's having instead of…" Before I could finish talking Ma said, "She'll have lemonade, thank you." Nicole laughed and said, "Yes ma'am." Now I know I'm old enough to have me a glass of wine, but that's the downside of loving being spoiled by your parents. You are always a baby and you can't pick and choose when you'll be a baby. I can get me some wine later when Sammi comes, right now I'll enjoy me some "lemonade that cool refreshing drink."

I couldn't help but sing it the way Eddie Murphy did in

his *"Delirious"* comedy stand up show impersonating Elvis. Lamar and I had watched it as children at our Uncle John's house; my daddy would have a fit if he knew that had happened. We were not allowed to watch anything with cursing in it, nowadays that is almost impossible. Uncle John would say, "That was good cussing T.V. This mess now is reality fake." Uncle John was so funny. He died last year in a motorcycle accident. It tore my daddy up, and I had a hard time with it, too. I think what hurt Daddy the most was that Uncle John never accepted Jesus Christ as his personal Lord and Savior; at least not openly. He was in a coma for two days before he died, Mama told Daddy that Uncle John could have surrendered his life to God. She said, "Keep living holy and see if your little brother is there."

Meanwhile, as Mama and I were getting our mani's and pedi's, we talked about the poem I would be reading at my commencement service. She asked, "Baby girl have you written your poem yet?" I told her, "Yes ma'am, I will let you review it once we get back to the hotel." I always let Mama read over my poetry, or the songs I wrote. I had once thought about being a writer, and Mama would always tell me, "Girl this is where you gift is. God has anointed you to write." I don't know about it being anointed, but it is what got me through college. I wrote so many essays for scholarships that it became effortless, and writing paid for my degree.

The relaxation was over, Mama paid and tipped, and we headed back to the hotel. As we walked back all we could discuss was how nice the Massage Green Spa was, and we compared it to Day Dreams Day Spa in Winterville. We didn't discuss Edward on the way back either.

Lamar had just pulled up in front of the hotel and was getting out of his car so the valet could take it. "Look Mama, it's Lamar and Sammi!" I screamed and ran to Lamar, "Hey big brother," and hugged him. "Hey Lil Ma, what's up?" Lamar called me Lil Ma since I was ten years old. He said it was because I thought I was his mama. I looked over at Sammi and screamed again, "S to the A to the M M I! What's up?" I shouted. She replied back just like I knew she would, "T to the A to the Ma R A! You go baby, graduating in two days." Sammi and I were certain that we were going to be the next great MC female rap duo. I would write most of the lyrics and Sammi had that smooth MC Lyte voice. We had so much fun and even entered a few talent shows. Needless to say, we ain't controlling no mics. Sammi works for some big insurance company, and I'm about to graduate without a job.

CHAPTER FOUR

Lamar & Sammi

Lamar looked at Mama and said, "Sexy mama." She blushed every time he said that and her reply was always, "Oh stop boy, you're a piece of work!" They had been going through that little skit for the past five years. Then she quickly changed the subject and asked, "Did you take care of all the orders before you left, lock up the building good and cut on the alarms?" She was asking about Clean Shine; Mama was indeed about her and Daddy's business. He told her, "Yes Mama, I got this. Stop stressing, and let me do me." Without missing a beat, she said "Boy please; I'm just making sure I don't have to fire you, and you have to do you somewhere else." Then she winked at him and as we were getting on the elevator looked at Sammi and said, "Hello Samantha, how are you? You didn't try to seduce my son on the way here did you?" Mama was always on Sammi about Lamar. I don't know if she even knew that the reason they broke up was because Lamar tried to get Sammi into bed.

She didn't dislike Sammi, but she loved her only begotten son and she didn't think anyone was good enough for him. Sammi just smiled and said with such poise, "Hey Mrs. Daniels, ain't nobody trying to get Lamar. Give me a hug." Mama laughed and gave her a hug and said, "How you doing sweetie? What have you been up to?" Mama did love Sammi. Sammi said, "Oh just working crazy hours. I found a church and I am thinking about joining." Sammi knew the best way to get on Mama's good side was to talk about going to church, or ask her a question about the Bible. Lamar knew what was up and that Mama was getting ready to start a sermon, so he quickly said, "Mama where's Pops?" I thought to myself, "Thank you Jesus, because she was gone make sure Sammi got the third degree about that church, and its pastor." Mama told Lamar that Daddy was upstairs in the suite sleeping and Lamar said, "Time for him to get up." The elevator doors opened just in time because Mama was looking at Sammi again ready to find out just what church she was thinking about joining.

Sammi and I walked ahead of Lamar and Mama. They had a business-related conversation going, and I was glad, it gave me time to talk to Sammi about Edward.

Sammi asked, "Tamara, what's up with Edward? Where is he? I thought for sure he was going to be smothering you and I wasn't going to get any girl time with you." I replied as my eyes began to tear up, "Sammi, I don't know if I'm getting married. I haven't talked to him in two days; things got ugly about you know what." "Really Tamara? Do you think that he waited all this time, only to get mad thirty days before your wedding about sex? So y'all really didn't do it yet?" I looked at her with disbelief that she would ask me such a question. I replied, "No, what do you mean? You're still a virgin, right?" We were walking and talking. I hadn't noticed where we were. Mama interrupted, "Tamara, where are y'all going?" We were passing our suite, I said, "Oh my bad, we're here." When we walked in Daddy was sitting at the table eating a bowl of ice cream and said, "When are we going to eat?"

Lamar greeted Daddy, "What's up Big Papa?" Daddy replied with questions just like Mama. "Hey son, did you take care of all the orders before you left, lock up the building good and cut on the alarms?" Sammi, mama, and I started laughing. I bet Lamar wasn't going to tell Daddy the same thing he told Mama. Lamar said, "Yes sir, and I double checked," and that was all he said. Daddy said, "Good job, you remind me of your daddy." My daddy was so corny, but that was one of the reasons I loved him so much. Mama said, "If you all get cleaned up we can head to dinner." I wasn't hungry, but Lamar and Daddy clearly were because they both said in unison, "Good."

I was glad that Lamar went to him and Edward's room to get ready. Mama and Daddy were getting ready in their room, which left me and Sammi alone to talk while we were in our room getting ready. I started the conversation, "Sammi, why would you ask me if I'm still a virgin? Aren't you?"

CHAPTER FIVE

Liars Liars

Sammi never gave me a straight answer, and Mom was yelling, "Let's go girls; Have you all decided where you want to go to eat?" Everyone knew my favorite restaurant was Bahama Breeze, which was about five minutes away from the college. Daddy was more of a burger and steak man, so I waited to see what he was going to say. "I would like to go somewhere and get me a thick juicy steak," which was fine with me too. So, I suggested my next favorite place to go, "Let's go to the Cheesecake Factory." Lamar always said that the Cheesecake Factory was for losers. That's because he was too cheap to take a date there. I'm sure since daddy was paying he would be fine.

I noticed he wasn't in the room yet so I asked, "Where's Lamar?" Sammi quickly said, "He's still in his room I'll get him, I need to get something out of his bag." "Okay good," I replied, that gave me time to change my shoes. I had on heels and I knew after we ate mama would want to go to the mall. Mama loved to shop, and since we didn't take Daddy up on his suggestion to go earlier without him, I knew that we would after dinner. Mama said, "Baby girl go and get

Lamar and Samantha and tell them let's go. Your father and I will be waiting."

When I walked across the hall to Lamar's room I tried to open the door, but it was locked. Good thing I had the extra card key. I put the key in, the lights on the panel turned green, I turned the knob, and pushed the door open. "Mama said let's go; what are y'all doing?" I asked Lamar and Sammi, they both looked a little culpable. My phone started playing: "And I am telling you, I'm not going..." It was Jennifer Hudson's version. I hurried and reached in my purse because I knew it was a text from Edward. I opened the text and it read: "Love you babe, and I miss you." I was eager to reply, but my pride wouldn't let me.

"Is that E?" Lamar asked. "Tell that fool he need to get here by 10:00 tonight, because its lights out after that. I'm tired." Sammi, Lamar, and I went down to join Mama and Daddy and then we all went to the Cheesecake Factory. We all ate, sat back, talked, and laughed, and when the check came everyone was quiet; because we knew what Daddy was going to say. "Y'all must be gone wash dishes; I ain't got this kind of money." He was so corny, and then he said as always, "I got two children, Lamar and Tamara. Who the heck is gratuity?" Then Daddy would laugh at his own corny jokes, and his loving wife laughed with him. Everyone was laughing! I don't know why Sammi and Lamar were laughing, but I was laughing because I didn't have any money. I'm going to laugh at every corny joke he tells, ALL THE TIME.

Sammi asked to be excused to go to the bathroom, AGAIN. I joked with her, "Dang girl, you got OAB (Over active bladder)?" She had been to the bathroom twice already.

I was thinking about Edward's text; "Love you, babe and I miss you." Why wasn't he apologizing for being a jerk? Why wasn't he calling instead of texting? I started getting mad again, but I thought about what Mama said on the way to the spa about not trying to analyze everything. I still was a bit perplexed by it all, but it was shopping time and I had just what I needed to shop...my daddy!

We were still walking and looking, when Daddy said, "Time to go. Everybody that's not in the truck when I get in it, must have other arrangements." We all knew what that meant, even Mama because Daddy had left us at the mall back home before. We were walking behind Daddy, and Sammi again had to go to the bathroom. I told her, "Girl you better come on! My daddy will leave you right here." She insisted that she had to go, my advice to her was, "You should really get that checked or get some depends." Lamar said, "You corny just like your daddy; go and stall Pops and I'll wait with her."

Daddy liked watches, and we were passing through Macy's so I said, "Look daddy at these MK watches." He stopped and looked, and then he said, "What's a MK watch?" "Michael Kors Daddy," I answered back. He looked at the watch and then asked the sales lady to pull it out for him to have a closer look. As he examined the watch he moaned and said how nice it was, and then he looked at the price tag... He shouted, "$250.00!" Mama said to the sales lady, "Just put it back up sweetie, before he has a heart attack." Daddy always made comments like that, knowing he could afford stuff, just being cheap.

We were all laughing, and I saw Sammi and Lamar coming, so I started walking towards the exit and shaking my head. "Daddy you are a trip." Lamar asked, "What Pops did now?" Lamar's phone rang and he answered, so no one responded to his question. Daddy was talking to Mama, and Sammi and I started talking. We were all in the truck and I heard Lamar say, "E are you sure? ...yeah, yeah, I got you." I wanted to know so bad if he was talking to Edward. Why was Edward calling Lamar and not me? This negro got me messed up. I was at it again, now I was analyzing Lamar's phone call. I was stressing...we pulled up to the hotel and I said, "I'm going swimming." I knew that would give me a chance to calm down and not allow my family to see me upset. Sammi decided to go swimming with me, I was glad because she and I needed to talk.

The pool was beautiful. There was a fireplace, private areas with gazebo tents with loungers inside, and the water felt great. It wasn't cold or hot, it was just right. I thought this might have been a mistake; Edward was all in my head. I swam a few laps and then stopped to look for Sammi, she was in the jacuzzi. "Come swim with me Sammi," I yelled at her. I knew she wouldn't, so I got out of the pool and went and got in the jacuzzi with her. I stepped in and said, "Girl this water is hot, too hot." Sammi said, "It's so relaxing." She was right, after just sitting there for a minute I could feel my body calming down. Now was the perfect time for me to talk to Sammi about Edward. "Sammi," I said "So Edward and I haven't talked since Monday and today is Wednesday. He was pressuring me about sex, and I told him we're getting married in less than a month. I'm puzzled at his behavior. Do you think that he has hooked up with someone else?" She said, "Stop being dramatic, you always go overboard." "What do you mean overboard?" I asked.

Sammi said to me, "You have a good man Tamara, one that loves you and wants to marry you. Stop being that nagging woman that sends the man to the rooftop." I asked her, "What the heck are you talking about?" I had heard Mama say something like that before, but where was Sammi coming from? "I've been going to church lately I heard the preacher say something like that. If you're a wife that gets on your husband's nerves, that he would rather sit on the top of the house than hear your mouth." My comeback was, "I'm gone have to look that up." "Look it up," she said. "Girl I just want August 30th to come so we can go ahead and get married, then I'm gone do flips for that negro, but not until we say our vows and the preacher says: I now pronounce you man and wife." It was hot in the jacuzzi, so I had to get out. Sammi had her eyes closed and looked deep in thought. "I'm going up to the room, are you coming Sammi?" "No you go ahead, I'm going to stay here and relax for a little while longer, and then I'll be up." My girl works so many hours at her job, this was kind of a vacation for her, so I said, "Okay," and headed up to the room. I wanted to check my phone to see if Edward had tried to contact me.

When I got up to the room door I prayed, "God please don't let my mama and daddy be in here doing nothing a child don't want to hear their parents doing." So, I knocked on the door very lightly, and then knocked on Lamar's door across the hall. Lamar opened the door to let me in and walked back to watch the TV. We both sat there quiet for a while, then he looked up and said, "Where's Sammi?" I told him that she stayed down to the jacuzzi. "Can I ask you a question Lamar?" I asked. "What's up Lil Ma?" "Has Edward said anything to you about how he feels about me right now?" Lamar looked at me, "That negro in love, he whipped." I responded anxiously, "No he ain't whipped. There's been none of that going on. Edward has never touched me. I could be a man and he doesn't even know." Then my brother said something that was like music to my ears, "I know sis, that's why I say he's whipped. You got game because Edward is crazy about you, and I know for a fact that he really respects the fact that you haven't given in to his weaknesses." I told him that we haven't talked for two days. "Stop tripping Lil Ma, I'm going to go take a dip in the pool." He was in the bedroom changing his clothes and I yelled, "Will you go in our suite first and make sure the coast is clear? Your parents are freaks and I don't want to walk in on them." He came out the bathroom and laughed. "You're crazy girl, come on." So, he led the way, and I made sure to walk behind him as he opened the door. I went directly to my room. I shouted as he was leaving out, "Thanks bro."

I jumped in the shower and sang all my favorite songs by Whitney Houston. "I'm every woman it's all in me... How will I know if he really loves me...All at once...Didn't we almost have it all...I'm your baby tonight...Where do broken hearts go..." I was depressing myself. I thought about Sammi and that she didn't have a key so I hurried out of the shower. Once I got out I grabbed my phone, and I texted Edward: I love and miss you too, Babe. I sat there with a towel on and thought about skyping him. No, I better not. Tempting him will only make things worse, plus I was feeling like a Jezebel. I was sitting on my bed and heard noises; I hoped it wasn't my parents going at it. I started singing to tune it all out and I put on a pair of sweat pants and a t-shirt and went across to Lamar's room. I went in, but he wasn't there. I thought to myself, "He must still be at the pool." I walked to the elevator to go to the pool, when I got on the elevator there was this cute couple holding hands and kissing. I couldn't help but think about how Edward and I always held hands when went out.

I walked to the pool area and didn't see Lamar, so I walked over to the Jacuzzi. He and Sammi weren't there either. I hoped I hadn't missed them between elevators because she will have to wait in Lamar's room until I came back up. I wanted to get me a drink so I walked over to the soda machine by the gazebos and heard a familiar voice.

"I love you Lamar." It was Sammi, so I peaked in the gazebo and saw my brother and Sammi almost naked and kissing. It was not a holy kiss either. Lamar replied, "I love you too, and everything will be okay, I promise. We will tell everyone later, after Lil Ma graduation. This is her weekend."

Tell everyone what? Are they back together? Why are they being so secretive about being together? I would love for them to be together so Sammi could be my sister in law, and they have me some little nieces and nephews. Maybe they are concerned about Mama, but she only be playing with Sammi and Lamar knows that. I tipped toed back to the door and opened it as I sang loud so they would hear me coming. The only song that popped in my head to sing was: "Secret lovers, that's what we are…" "Tamara," Sammi was calling me to the gazebo. "Where you at girl?" I played dumb. She stepped out and I saw her. As I walked towards her I said, "Oh this is nice, looks like a good place for couples to snuggle and hide from everyone; is it roomy?" I asked as I pushed her aside to see my brother. That negro was ghost! He must have gone out the back; I noticed there was an opening. The next thing I heard was water splash, "Lil Ma, you had to get away from Ma and Pops?"

I walked out the gazebo and saw Lamar swimming across the pool. I stood there looking flabbergasted, and Sammi must have noticed because she said, "He's been jumping off that diving board and into the pool almost the entire time he's been down here." "And jumping on you the other time," is what I was thinking. How ya'll gone try to play me?" "I didn't see you when I came out here," I shouted across the pool to Lamar. He yelled back, "That's because you thought you were in concert singing." Then he jumped in again.

So they gone play me like monopoly? Really! Wow! These liars, right in my face. I wondered if Sammi had given in to Lamar. She assured me they were done and now they're talking about I love you. Sammi was just talking about church, and putting a brother on the roof top because you're getting on his nerves. I guess she figured out how to keep him in the house. Okay, I'll play along with their little game. This is childish, but… Game on!

I walked next to Lamar while he was swimming, "Let's race Ma." Lamar and I raced. He swam and I ran on the pool deck. We always had some silly kind of competition going. Once he was done and got out of the pool we sat in front of the fireplace with Sammi and just talked about old times. Yeah these liars thought I was going to leave them alone to enjoy that nice romantic setting. NOT GONE HAPPEN!!!

I figured I would say something to get a reaction out of Sammi, "Lamar, I want you to meet my girl Myesha, she's really pretty and very nice." I looked at Sammi, "And I want you to meet Chase, he's Jamaican, and too fine for words. He's Morris Chestnut and Taye Diggs mixed all up together. If Edward wasn't so fine, Chase would be the one." So, both these fools sitting here looking like I just rained on their parade. I stood and said, "Let's go. I'm tired." BAM! That's what they get, trying to play me.

We were getting on the elevator, and they were still speechless. I'm singing my boy Anthony Hamilton's song, "No matter what the people say, I can't let go..." Ya'll must have had a peanut butter sandwich, y'all ain't saying any-thing." I teased with them. I got no reply. "Y'all gone have the stank breath," I was laughing so hard inside; Lamar looked at me and rolled his eyes so hard. "What's that look for bro?" I asked. "You're so loud; I thought you said you were tired." He muttered kind of annoyed with me. I didn't say anything because I was tired and sleepy, but tomorrow - - game on for real. I was planning to get Myesha and Chase to play along. Sammi and I went to our room, and Lamar went into his. I guess it was lights out and Edward hadn't made it yet. Where was he?

Sammi lay down on her bed- (now I know this skank gone wash her stank behind). "Umm, you plan on showering? You got all that nasty chlorine on you." She looked at me and replied, "Yeah girl, I was just thinking." I was eager to hear about what, but she got up and went to shower. While Sammi was showering, I thought how disappointed I was with my best friend and my brother, but they weren't doing anything that Edward and I hadn't done. They kissed, so what, and said they loved each other, so what. I was judging them, and that was wrong. She shouldn't tempt him, just like I shouldn't have tempted Edward. I guess I was mad cause AIN'T NOBODY TOLD ME NOTH-ING!!!

I picked up my phone to text Myesha and Chase and noticed I had missed Edward's call and two text messages. Excited, I listened to my voicemail. "Hey babe, I love you, I miss you, and I'm so ready for you to be Mrs. Edward Curtis Wilcox. See you tomorrow." My heart fluttered and I was blushing like a high school girl. I scrolled to my text messages to read, "Hey babe, can't make it tonight, be there tomorrow by two." That's cool, I can wait until two. The next message read: "Hey babe, change of plans, I'll be there by noon." I was ecstatic; I couldn't wait to tell Sammi, but first, I had to text Edward back.

"Hey my chocolate truffle, I love you too and miss you more. I've been going crazy not being able to talk to you." I pressed send, and then I laid there thinking how desperate that sounded. "And I am telling you..." he was texting me right back. "Stop going crazy, I'm in love with you, girl. Now go to bed, it's late and I want to make it there to you by noon. Love you, babe, goodnight."

I was smiling from ear to ear and I was on cloud nine.

I went to the bathroom door, "Sammi, Sammi, are you okay?" I opened the door and she was not in the bathroom. She was not in the room at all, and I noticed the key to our room was gone. I went across to Lamar's room and let myself in; it was dark so I used the light from my cell phone to see my way to the bedroom. There it was. No more judging. Lamar and Sammi were doing what only married folk ought to be doing. I let myself back out and went to our room. I was seriously thinking about waking up my Mama and telling her, but I didn't. I just texted Myesha and Chase and told them what I needed them to do tomorrow, and to meet us for breakfast at Mimi's Café. Because Daddy and I loved to get the Cinnamon Brioche French Toast, and Mama loved the Strawberry Waffle Perdu, I knew it wouldn't be a problem getting everyone to agree with eating there. Plus, I had to have them play games before Edward came. He didn't like me being messy, and that was what I was planning to be. I know it's childish, but I can't help it…

CHAPTER SIX

Messy Surprise

It was Thursday, July 31st, 5:00 a.m. when I woke up. I don't know when Sammi came back, but Mama woke us up like she used to do me and Lamar. "This is the day the Lord has made, let us rejoice and be glad in it." I heard that my whole life. "Get up, time to meet with Jesus," she would say. I remember one morning Lamar said, "Jesus still sleep Ma," and she slapped him and said, "This is not a time for play." After that we got on up, because Mama meant business when it came to God. "Go get your brother Baby Girl." As I was going across the hall, I reminisced about how I joked with Lamar about mama slapping him for playing. I told him, "Lamar you better get up or Mama gone come and slap the hell out you again." No sooner than I said it, I turned around and I got slapped in the mouth! Mama said, "This is not a time for play." So, if we didn't learn anything else we learned one thing for sure: don't play on God's time because mama will slap the hell out of you. I reached Lamar's room and went in, "Get up big head, Mama said it's time to pray." Lamar got his butt up and came right on, clearly he remembers too. We didn't get to brush our teeth or nothing; we just hurried to pray so she didn't have to come get us.

We all prayed, and as mad as I was with Lamar and Sammi, that was their business, so I didn't tell Mama, but I was still gone play games. Mama said, "I guess I'll cook breakfast." Daddy and Lamar were glad about that. "No!" I shouted. Everybody looked at me as if I had lost my mind. "Please Daddy! I've been wanting some Cinnamon Brioche French Toast from Mimi's Café, it's right on River Coast Drive." "Oh that does sound good Baby Girl." Daddy agreed, and Mama chimed in too, "Yes, I can get me some of that delicious Strawberry Waffles Perdu. So, let's get dressed and we can go." By the time everyone got dressed, I texted Edward and told him that we were going to breakfast at Mimi's Café, and I had graduation practice at 11 a.m., but should be back to the hotel by noon. Then, I texted Myesha and Chase and told them that we were planning to get to breakfast about 9:00 a.m. They both texted me the same reply: "You owe me for this." I didn't want to talk smack, but I started to reply: "Ya'll broke butts owe me." I'll tell 'em later.

"Sammi, girl Chase is gone be so happy to meet you, and I think you two will hit it off. He goes to church; I know you into that churchy don't send your man to the rooftop thang now. I guess Mrs. Clause nag, nag, nag, cause Santa goes from roof to..." "Tamara," Mama interrupted and looked at me and her eyes said "I'm about to slap you," so I shut up. Lamar looked at me and laughed and whispered so Mama wouldn't hear him, "She just looked the hell outta you." Then he called me corny out loud so he could justify his laughter. I looked at him and said, "Myesha isn't corny, she's smart and she even wears her own hair." Lamar hated weave. We pulled up to Mimi's Café and I saw Myesha's car, so I knew they were already inside.

We walked inside and the waitress sat us. I didn't see Myesha or Chase. The waitress came up and said, "I'm Deedee. I'll be your server for the evening. May we start with your drinks or do you wish to have time to consider?" Daddy said "I'm ready, I'll have..." he stopped talking because he noticed some jerk doing tricks on a motorcycle in the parking lot. Daddy didn't like to see people doing stunts on motorcycles ever since his brother Uncle John died. Then my friends walked up and I introduced them. After everyone sat down, Mama apologized to the server and continued with our drink orders. The table we were at had extra seats, so it was time to get messy. I started giving instructions, "Lamar, why don't you sit by Myesha, and Chase, you can sit by Samantha." Then I heard a voice say, "And I will sit right here next to you."

I looked around with a grin on my face knowing that it was my chocolate truffle. Mm mm mm, this negro is so dang on fine, my entire body trembled. "Hey beautiful." It was Edward. "Hey babe," I said in an innocent, yet sexy voice. I stepped into his arms to hug him and give him a big, long, wet kiss and he pecked me and said, "Hello Ma & Pop Daniels, how are you?" My parents were blocking; ain't nobody block them last night. I wanted to kiss my man, the way I wanted to kiss him. For the next two minutes, it was meet and greet, and then we sat down and looked through the menu. I was so happy that Edward was there that I hadn't noticed that Myesha and Chase were not sitting next to Lamar and Sammi as I instructed earlier before Edward came. There was no way I was about to start any mess now. So, if my plan happens, it must be all Myesha and Chase. No one was talking, just looking over the menu. Edward and I were holding hands and smiling like teens. I love this man.

Once we were done eating, Mama, Daddy, Sammi, and Lamar left together to go back to the hotel. Edward and I stood outside and chatted with Myesha and Chase for a while, and then Edward went to get his car. I loved watching him walk. I had a big kool-aid smile watching him.

CHAPTER SEVEN

All About Edward

"You two are losers," I joked with Myesha and Chase. They didn't do anything that we discussed, I guess they couldn't. "Sorry, maybe you should stay out of peoples' business," Myesha suggested. I kind of looked at her and rolled my eyes, but this day was all about Edward, and I wasn't trying to get mad about anything. Plus, she was right.

Myesha and Chase were still talking, but I was in my own world with thoughts. I wanted Edward and me to go for a swim, to go shopping, to go to the movies, and to have a serious talk about our recent argument. Should I just forget that he tripped with me about something we clearly had an understanding about? Is he going to want to go to the roof top because he thinks I'm nagging about it? I know we aren't my parents, but we need to have "Settlement Table" going into our new relationship as husband and wife. I felt awful those few days that we had no communication after a disagreement. "Tamara, Tamara, girl we're leaving. Talk to you later."

I stood and waitied while Edward was pulling up in his black 2007 Cadillac CTS. He had on a pair of dark Armani shades, and looked so good. He parked and stepped out the car. I hadn't noticed his attire. He had on a Polo shirt, a pair of blue jeans, and a pair of brown and black Polo boots. Yeeessss! Edward was about swag and he knew he looked good. I saw a few of the other ladies observing him as he was walking towards me. So, I started walking to meet him, serving notice to them all--he's all about me. Once we met we greeted one another with open arms as if we hadn't seen one another, and he picked me up to him and I kissed him. He put me down and I looked at him and said, "I love you, babe." He smiled, grabbed my hand and we started walking to his car.

Edward was the type of guy that still opened car doors, and I was so proud to be with him. When he opened my door, before I got in I kissed him again, and this time I put my hands on his face and closed my eyes. That's the way I wanted to kiss him when he first arrived at Mimi's. It was short, but unquestionably passionate. When the kiss was over I got in the car. Edward closed the door and then he walked around to the driver side. I looked over at Myesha and she threw me thumbs up. I smiled and let the window down, I'll see you tomorrow girl. Then I decided to get her and Chase going and screamed, "My Wings 2008," and they both chanted back, "Soaring high cause we are great." I'm so excited about graduation tomorrow; I know we're going to be outrageously crazy.

I let the window back up and looked at Edward; he had a smirk on his face. "What, babe?" I asked. "Why are you smiling?" He called me corny, and insisted that it was funny watching me act flamboyant. I just laughed because we still had a lot of learning to do of one another. Mama said that she and Daddy are still learning things about each other, so that did not discourage me. "So what do you want to do babe?" I asked Edward. He looked at me and said, "You, but I can wait." I'm glad that was his answer so I could bring up the argument. "So why did you get mad Monday, and not contact me for two days?" All he said was, "I'm sorry, but I'm flesh and bones and I did not want to speak to you wrong or have an attitude with you." Then I asked him, "So you make me suffer by not calling, texting, or contacting me in any way?" "That's not fair Edward, and I want us to come up with a fair way to disagree with one another." He returned a sincere apology, "Baby I'm sorry, but you just don't know how bad I want to make love to you." He just doesn't know how bad I want him to make love to me. "Edward, yes I am a virgin but I still desire to be with you because I love you, but I want to wait until I am your wife. I believe God will bless our marriage for that reason alone." He said with a serious look on his face, "Okay, but you need to stop being fine until our wedding day." We both laughed, and I sang with the song playing on the radio: "Baby since the day you came into my life, you made me realize that we were born to fly," by John Legend. I love John Legend as much as Anthony Hamilton; I will most certainly have their music in my wedding.

I wanted Edward and me to go do something romantic, like walk around the lake or go to see *27 Dresses*, at the movies, but he suggested that we start packing up stuff and getting rid of junk that I don't want from my dorm room. He still was in amazement that I lived on campus my entire four years of college, and did it without a car. My parents said they were not getting me an apartment, which would help cut back on fornication, at least that is what Mama would always say. I knew lots of people that were not deterred by living on campus, but for me I guess she was right because I am still pure. I'm kind of proud of myself the more I think about it, but I'm ready to get married. I have heard so many things about sex, and I am very curious to find them out; I'll admit I'm nervous too. Edward and I talked about a few things, but because we both seem to be in heat right now and it is so close to our wedding day, I will wait to ask him more questions, or better yet he can teach me.

"So what are we doing?" I asked. He was pulling into the hotel. He said, "I want to get changed, grab Lamar and Sammi, and we need to go back and start packing up your stuff." I replied, "No, babe we can chill today. We will have another four days after graduation to get that stuff." "Tamara," he never calls me by name unless he wants me to stop and listen. "Lamar has to get back to work, and I have to get back to work, your mom and pops will be here and I don't want to put all of that lifting on your pops." I hadn't thought about Lamar and Edward leaving Sunday night, a few days before the rest of us. I guess I had to be grateful that he was thinking about Daddy. I suppose he's right, so we went up to get changed into some work clothes and to get Lamar and Sammi.

Once we got to the suite room doors, he walked in with me; my mama and daddy were sitting there eating ice-cream. Edward sat down with them and mama asked Edward if he wanted some, of course he said yes. I walked into Sammi's and my room and she wasn't there. "I'll be back," I said as I walked out the door and across the hall. I almost knew what I was about to walk in on, but I did it anyways. When I walked in there was no one in the TV area, so I walked in the bedroom, again I saw no one, but I heard water running in the bathroom. I walked to the bathroom door, which was not shut and peeked in; Sammi and Lamar were taking a shower together. I also noticed a box on the bathroom counter, it was a pregnancy test. OMG! Is Sammi pregnant? I left without saying a word. This is too much boiling inside of me! I gotta tell somebody. This is messing up my weekend! There is a chance that I'm going to be an aunt soon! Yes, this is messing up my weekend.

I walked back across the hall and my parents and Edward were still eating ice-cream. I mumbled, "I'm going to get changed babe and then we can go to the college." The look on my face must have caused concern because Edward asked me if I was okay; I just kept walking and did not reply. While I was in the room changing, I heard the door opening, it was Sammi. I was so pissed off that she was keeping this from me, because I tell Sammi everything. I thought she told me everything. Clearly, she doesn't. Seeing her and Lamar in the shower was intense for me. I know I'm not a child, but I feel like a little kid that caught her big brother doing something appalling. I was shocked. Sammi said, "What's up girly?" I looked at her and she was acting normal, like nothing had even happened. I wonder how many times they have done this. I replied, "Not much, you smell so fresh and so clean. Where you been at?" I felt so foolish once it came out my mouth, I sounded like an adolescent. I was being stupid, so before she had a chance to respond I quickly interrupted saying, "We're just gonna get sweaty moving and cleaning my dorm room." She looked a little puzzled, but brushed it off and said, "No problem, but you better be glad I love you like a sister." We laughed and walked out the room. SMH and thinking, "Love me like a sister nothing. THAT MAKES LAMAR YOUR BROTHER, NASTY!!!"

Lamar was finishing up a bowl of ice-cream; he must have come over while Sammi and I were in the room. I commented, "Every time I turn around one of ya'll eating ice-cream." Of course, my smart mouth mama replied, "That's why I bought it, to be eaten. What is your problem?" I didn't respond, I just grabbed my purse and headed to the door. Edward, Lamar, and Sammi got up to follow, and I heard Mama say something about take your time and do a good job, but as soon as we were done and came back we could all go to the movies. She wanted to see The Mummy: Tomb of Dragon Emperor. I didn't want to go to the movies because there was so much going on in my head. Yeah right, "take your time" she says. I'm sure Mama and Daddy are glad we're all leaving. I'M SURROUNDED BY FREAKS.

Daddy had designated Lamar to take my stuff back to Winterville, so when we got down to the cars Lamar attached the 4' x 8' U-Haul cargo trailer to his car. Edward and I got in his car, and Sammi rode with Lamar. I wanted to tell Edward about Lamar and Sammi so bad, but what if he feels that we should be doing what they are doing. I was silent the entire ride to the college. I cannot believe that Sammi could be pregnant from my brother. Mama gonna go slap off. Wow! Why did Sammi let Lamar talk her into the bed? She and I had planned to save our bodies until marriage. We had been planning this since we were in 6th grade, and I know we were both still virgins when we graduated from high school. Now she may be pregnant. Lord have mercy. This is so devastating for me. A baby, that reason alone was enough for me to not take the risk.

Mama said something to me before about how a mistake can feel good for a few minutes, but it will last a lifetime. I was praying to God that she didn't mean that sex only felt good for a few minutes, but the bigger picture that I think she was trying to get me to understand was not doing it God's way could result in a lifelong mistake. Thinking about Sammi and Lamar situation, if she is pregnant a child will be in their life forever, and they will be connected for a lifetime. What if they don't want to be together? Now they have put an innocent baby in a dysfunctional situation, because of their lust. Mama gonna preach kingdom come to them, and then Edward and I will have to hear it too, and get oil slapped across our heads. I want to drop kick the both of them.

Finally, we made it to the college and Edward came around to open my door. Before he let me out he asked, "Baby what's wrong?" I knew this was not the time to share, so I just kissed him and told him I loved him and that he meant so very much to me. He grabbed my hand, gave me a kiss, and said, "Come on, let's go clean your mess." I laughed and told him it wasn't that bad. I was trying to see what Sammi and Lamar were up to as Lamar parked. They were just jamming to some song on the radio; it sounded like Christian rap. These phonies doing the nasty one minute and listening to Christian music the next. Wow! Let me stop judging.

We all got up to my dorm room and I said, "See, I told y'all it wasn't that bad." I had been packing for the past two weeks. I had a refrigerator, TV, stereo, clothes, shoes, and other odds and ends. I don't know why Mama rented that big cargo trailer; she could have rented a smaller one. The most of our time would be consumed in cleaning the room, and then I could turn in the key. I'm kind of glad Edward suggested we do this today, because now I don't have to come back after the commencement service.

Edward and Lamar both had on tank tops, and I saw Myesha and some other ladies looking at them as they were loading up the U-haul with the mini refrigerator. I laughed, because I was sure Myesha was telling them about my ridiculous plan for her and Chase to play with Lamar and Sammi. I am glad the plan didn't work; it seems there is more to Sammi and Lamar than I thought, and I would never do anything to hurt either of them.

Sammi and I were talking about old times and cleaning, reminiscing on how my parents wouldn't allow me to go spend the night over to her house, but when she stayed over to our house she had to help me clean up. "Girl you remember your mama use to make a song out of everything?" She said laughing and holding her belly. I couldn't help but think about the pregnancy test I saw in the bathroom in Lamar and Edward's room, but I didn't want to talk about it now so I replied, "She still do." We cleaned and laughed as the men continued moving the bigger things out and then down into the cargo trailer. I looked out the window of my dorm room and noticed Myesha and the other ladies standing down by the U-haul. Now I'm fine as wine, so other women don't generally threaten me, but these chics got nerve. Almost everyone knew I was a virgin, so parading in front of my man with short-shorts on kind of upset me. Myesha and I were okay, but nothing like Sammi and I. Would she dare try Edward?

Sammi and I just watched for a while, then Sammi said, "I told you I didn't like her," and then we went down. "Hey babe," I said to Edward. He bent down and kissed me saying, "Hey babe." Yeeeessss! I love this man. I had the mop in one hand and the bucket in my other hand, and Sammi had a bag of trash and the broom. I handed Myesha the mop and said, "You can have this, he's mine." She started to say something, but Sammi interrupted and said, "You can have this too, TRASH!" and she dropped the bag in front of her. We both left and went back inside, and didn't look back. I heard Edward and Lamar behind us, I would have been mad if they weren't. Lamar said, "Ya'll still think ya'll the Ali sisters." We laughed and I said, "We don't fight no more." I looked at the room, it was all clean. I told them I was going to turn in the key and would meet them at the car.

When I got down to admissions to turn in my key I saw Willie. Willie had been flirting with me every day for the past three years, and I have never given him the time of day. I must admit the attention he gave me was very affirming, and he was fine. "Okay Sexy T," Willie said, "This may be the last time I see you. May I please have a hug and a little kiss on the cheek?" I heard a voice, "I got your hug—and all her kisses belong to me," I turned around and saw Edward standing there. I smiled and introduced the two of them, "Willie, this is my fiancé Edward, which I've told you about several times." Willie looked Edward straight in his face and said, "I'm glad to finally meet the lucky man that hooked Sexy T. I was praying you didn't exist or you messed up before we graduated." OMG, I can't believe he said that, Edward is going to explode. Edward shook his hand and said, "Blessed man, blessed." Kissed me and we started walking off, and then Edward turned around and said to Willie, "Check yourself Bro." Edward has a temper, but he's never tripped in front of me, so I looked at him with disappointment. He knew it and tried to turn the tables and said, "What you mad because I checked your on-campus boyfriend?" I again looked at him with displeasure, and I said, "Really Edward, you're going to try to trip about nothing. He means nothing to me." He said, "I'm sorry, but you know I'll mess him up right?" We laughed and got in the car.

Lamar and Sammi were already in Lamar's car, again listening to music. I'm finding myself so consumed in them. I need to let it go and focus on myself. I just couldn't get pass seeing them in the shower together, but it really wasn't my business.

When we returned to the hotel and walked inside, we saw Mama and Daddy walking towards the elevator with swimsuits on; they had been to the pool. I wanted Edward and me to go down to the pool area and take advantage of the romantic scenery, but that just might be too much temptation for the both of us, so I didn't even suggest it. We hurried to catch up with Mama and Daddy so we could all get on the elevator together. Ma asked, "So are we going to the movies?" No one said anything; I guess we were all tired. I suggested that we stay in, order pizza, and watch a movie on TV. I wanted to see just what Lamar and Sammi did while the rest of the couples were all hugged up watching a movie. Lamar said, "I ain't trying to hang out with ya'll the whole time I'm up here. Ya'll rent a movie; I'm going bowling, to a comedy club, or something." Edward looked at me, and I said, "You can go; I want to hang out with Sammi anyways." Sammi blurted out, "I'm going too, and you stay here with your mama and daddy." Really!

So we all got dressed, excluding Mama and Daddy and ended up at The Comedy Zone. We didn't know who the comedian was, but his name was Reno Collier. He was "okay" funny, and it was something to do. We left there and went to Jax Lanes on Beach Blvd. It was fun, and we teamed up girls vs. boys. I was concerned for Sammi picking up the heavy bowling ball; I didn't want her to hurt herself if she was pregnant. After Sammi and I luckily beat Lamar and Edward, I said being facetious, "How about we couple up a game and see who wins. Lamar, you and Sammi can pretend to be a couple at least through one game, right?" They both looked very edgy, but Sammi said, "We can do that, it's on." Sammi and Lamar beat Edward and me, which didn't bother me, but Edward was so competitive. Knowing him like I did, I could tell he was upset a little, but he didn't let it show too much.

It was late and I was ready to go back to the hotel and lay it down, so I suggested that we go. When we got back Edward and I walked to the pool area. I figured we would be okay since we were fully dressed. When we walked in the fireplace was lit and the reflection from the fire on the pool water looked so idealistic for lovers to have a passionate moment. Edward stood in front of me and kissed me and said, "By this time next month you will be Mrs. Edward

Curtis Wilcox. I want you to know that I appreciate you making me wait and honor what you believe in. It has made me love you even more." I was in tears. Now I wanted to jump his bones and give him all of me, but I gave him a kiss and said, "Go to your room." I need to check my thoughts, the man trying to compliment me and these thoughts...

Sammi and Lamar was the last thing on my mind while Edward and I were together in the pool area, but on the way up to our rooms I thought that they are probably at it again. Then I thought about my parents being alone as well, and when we got to the room doors I didn't know which way to go. Edward kissed me and said, "I love you Sexy T." I guess that was his way of letting me know he hadn't forgot about Willie. We both smirked and went into our rooms. Mama and Daddy's door was open so I peeked in and they were both asleep. I then walked into my room not thinking Sammi was going to be there, but she was. She had already fallen asleep, so I quietly changed and got in the bed. As I laid there thinking about my day, I thanked God for blessing me and giving me strength to hold out. Mama was right when she said, "God is a keeper, if you want to be kept." I want to be kept, but my flesh is a mess.

CHAPTER EIGHT

Graduation Morning

It was 5:00 in the morning, on Friday, August 1st. "This is the day the Lord has made, let us rejoice and be glad in it." I heard Mama doing her wakeup call; "Get up, time to meet with Jesus." Sammi and I started getting up; I let her have the bathroom first, thinking about her situation. So, while she was using the bathroom, I went to wake up Edward and Lamar. I still had on my short sleep shorts and a tank top; of course, I brushed my hair back and gargled first. I knocked and then let myself in. I was headed straight to Edwards's room and noticed Mama was right behind me. She said, "Get your fast butt back over there and put on some clothes! I'll wake them." I replied like a little child caught in action, "Yes ma'am." Why she always acting like the police?

So, we were all there praying, just like always, but this morning was different. It was like worship service in the hotel room. Daddy prayed boldly, "God thank You for being God all by Yourself. Thank You for being all that we need, thank You for Your Son Jesus Christ dying on the cross so that we may live with You eternally. Thank You for allowing my baby to make it through college. Thank You Lord for the blessings You have bestowed upon us. Lord forgive us for our sins and lead us in the right direction. We praise You and You only Lord. Amen." I looked at Edward and he looked so serious. Sammi and Lamar looked serious too. What is going on here? Everyone chimed in together, "Amen."

I screamed, "Hallelujah Daddy, I'm graduating from college." He looked at me and smiled. It seemed as if he was a bit misty-eyed. I walked over to him and gave him a big hug and said, "Thank you Daddy." Mama and Sammi were both in the kitchen cooking. I thought they would have taken me out to breakfast on my big day, but oh well, I didn't have to help cook so I was okay. I asked Edward to listen to me practice my poem and tell me what he thought. After going over it a few times Mama called for us to come and eat, so of course everything was dropped and we all headed to the table.

Mama and Sammi had cooked eggs, bacon, grits, cinnamon toast, and cut up fresh fruit. It all looked good, but where did the food come from? I asked, "When y'all went to the grocery store?" Daddy said, "Your mother and I went when you all went to pack up your room." Edward said, "This is delicious Mrs. Daniels and Sammi." Lamar said, "It sure is Mama and Sammi." So, I said, "I don't care about the emphasis ya'll are putting on Mama and Sammi's name." Everyone laughed, and my daddy said, "But she smart and she sure can sing." "So everybody gone joke me on this very stressful day?" I had to put on the theatrics, because that's what I do. So then Mama said, "It's okay Baby Girl, you gone learn how to cook one day. Let's get ready to go to the salon and get your hair done."

Mama, Sammi, and I went to the salon, and my hairdresser Nichell put me right in the chair once I arrived. I hated waiting to get my hair done and Nichell knew it. Mama asked for an eyebrow arch for herself, she had a wig she was wearing and Sammi had micro braids in her hair. After we left the salon, we stopped by the gas station to get me some headache medicine. Mama said it was a nervous headache, and I'm sure she was right. I was panicky about today, and I think I was also a little nervous that my next big step would be marriage. Who gets married right after they graduate from college? "Hey Sexy T," I looked up; it was Willie. I smiled, and waved and kept walking. Sammi was waiting on a response, but I didn't say a word.

It wasn't a big deal. Willie and I were just friends and an explanation wasn't necessary. I thought that it was a bit weird that he did seem to make me smile every time he said hi to me. Is that a big deal? I wouldn't want a chick smiling every time Edward said hi. Is this an issue that needs to be addressed? OMG, why am I thinking about this? It's nothing. Thoughts were racing through my head that I did not have time to deal with right now.

CHAPTER NINE
Commencement Program

August 1, 2008, 3:00 p.m.

We took two vehicles to the ceremony, and once we arrived to the UNF Arena, Edward looked at me and said, "You are beautiful." I was so nervous, but I was ready to be done with college. Mama wanted me to get my Masters' Degree, but that's nowhere in my mind right now. I gave everyone a hug, kissed Edward and dashed off to the section where the scholars were instructed to meet. I walked in and saw Myesha. I hadn't spoken to her since I gave her the mop and told her Edward was mine. I saw Willie, he looked at me and we exchanged smiles. Am I flirting with him? I gotta stop this. I haven't given him the time of day and now I won't see him because he's going to the military and I'm going to Florida, not to mention getting married in less than a month. He started walking towards me and the officials started yelling, "Line up ladies and gentlemen; it's time for the ceremony to begin." I was so happy because I didn't mean to flirt with him. I would never cheat on Edward. I don't want to do anything that I wouldn't want Edward to do. This felt like cheating. OMG I'm so melodramatic. How do married people cheat for months and years without feeling guilty? Why is my mind here?

The music started playing, and tears started rolling down my face. I was so excited that graduation day had finally come. When I walked in I felt so proud. I saw my parents, Lamar, Sammi, and Edward to my left. I was very happy that they were here to share this milestone with me. Once everyone was in, we all sat down and the program started. As I sat and listened, I was thinking about my life. God has been good to me, and He deserves more of me. I plan to show God just how appreciative I am from this day forward. I am going to grow up and stop being such a big brat; I'm just going to be a little brat. I chuckled at myself. All I could do right now was say, "Thank you God for everything."

It was my time on the program to read my poem. I was selected to do this because I entered a poetry contest and won a scholarship, so the dean asked me to read it. I was scared to be standing in front of all those people, but I looked straight ahead and found a focus spot. My eyes were gazing into Willie's, and I began to recite my poem. I had memorized it word for word, and I looked at him the entire time I was speaking. Once I was done and realized I had been staring at Willie, I turned to look at Edward, and mouthed, "I love you." I hoped he didn't see me looking at Willie like a hawk. It was nothing. My speech professor said when speaking, find a focus point. What is my problem? What in the world is going on? I went back to my seat, and the roll call began.

"Tamara Monique Daniels," I didn't want my entire name called, but Mama wanted it, so it was my gift to her. By the time I made it across the stage and started walking down the steps, Edward was there with white roses in his hand. I had a smile on my face so big! I hugged him and gave him a peck on his cheek and I walked back to my seat. The last thing I heard was: "Congratulations Class of 2008." Caps flew up, but not mine. I wasn't trying to mess up my hair snatching that cap off!

Classmates were exchanging hugs, and tears were rolling down the faces of associates that knew this was more than likely the end of relationships. I was looking for my family and walked right into Willie. He smiled and said, "We did it." I agreed, "Yes we did." He held his arms wide, and I gave him a hug. I looked at him and asked, "Are you going to make the wedding?" His reply was crazy, "Or forever hold my peace." He walked away, and I turned around and saw my family. I knew that Mama had planned something special for me, so I was ready to see what she had put together.

CHAPTER TEN

Graduation Night

We all went to celebrate after the ceremony, and I was a little surprised to get outside and not see a brand-new car from Daddy and Mama. I am not going to be a brat about it because they were spending a lot of money on my wedding, so I should be an adult about this.

We ended up at my favorite place to eat, Bahama Breeze. Everyone ordered and we laughed and talked about everything we could talk about. Then Lamar said, "I have an announcement to make." Dang, is he going to just take my day away with whatever news him and Sammi have been hiding? "Baby Sis, I am so proud of you. You have graduated, you're getting ready to get married, and you did it all standing on what you believed in, and not falling for any tricks." So, I'm looking at him and thinking, "Too bad Sammi fell for your tricks." Then he said something that made my Mama cry out. "Mama, Daddy, I gave my life to Christ about a week ago." Now this negro was just getting his freak on yesterday, what is he up to? Then Sammi chimed in and said, "I also gave my life to Christ last week." I was thinking, "Oooh, Jesus okaying folks to get their freak on now?" So, Edward and I waiting for nothing…now they need to be ashamed of themselves. Then Lamar continued, "Sammi and I eloped in February."

Mama and Daddy were both smiling, Edward was smiling, and I blurted, "ELOPED! So ya'll have kept this from us for five months? Why?" Lamar said, "Because Ma and Pops were gone on their annual anniversary cruise to the Mediterranean for twenty-one days …." Then Sammi jumped in and said, "And you had turned down Edward on his proposal to elope last year, so we didn't want to make you feel like you should have." I was thinking, "So this heifer gone put my business out after she done clearly kept hers a secret?" I hadn't told my parents about Edward wanting to elope, and all they knew was that he asked them for my hand in marriage. Daddy and Mama swiftly looked at Edward and me, and Mama said, "What is this all about?" My reply was, "No! All eyes on them, this has nothing to do with us." Lamar said, "Look, we were trying to wait until the right moment, and things kept happening. The cruise, Edward proposed to you, Uncle John died, my promotion, and the graduation; so, we planned to wait until after the wedding…." I interrupted, "Whose wedding? Evidently not mine?"

Then Lamar shocked us all and said, "Sammi is a month pregnant." The look on Mama's face was pure delight. Daddy had that careless look on his face, and my entire demeanor change. I was excited about becoming an auntie. Edward somehow seemed very unruffled by anything that Lamar was saying. I'm sure he knew, and didn't tell me. So, he's keeping secrets, but I'm not going to trip. Not right now anyways.

It seemed like we all talked for hours about them being married, officially welcoming Sammi into the family, and baby names. I just wanted to know one thing; Was Sammi a virgin when they got married, and if so was it painful? I'm getting married, and nervous. I have talked to other girls before, but I knew Sammi would tell me the whole truth. However, did I want to hear about her and my brother? We agreed that we would share details with one another when we were younger, but I never thought she was going to marry Lamar, especially after they broke up. Mama always told me that being intimate for the first time with your husband was beautiful. She also said that she wasn't nervous, because she had done it the way God ordained it and she knew that God would bless her obedience. That's what I'm praying for, God to bless my obedience.

Mama looked at Sammi and said, "I thought you said you weren't trying to get my son." Sammi replied, "I already got him Ma Daniels." Everyone laughed. Then Daddy spoke, "Son, I am very proud of you. Treat her like a queen, love her like Christ loves the church..." Mama cut in and said, "That's Bible." Then Daddy continued, "Things won't always be easy, but God is able to get you through it and without Him you will fail." We all looked at Mama, and after about five seconds she said, "John 15:5." Yes, Mama was like a walking Bible. So, we laughed, and continued to chit chat and enjoy our dessert.

The server came and gave Daddy the check, Daddy said, "You can put his and hers together (pointing at Lamar and Sammi), and you can put his alone (pointing at Edward), and I will handle the three of us." We all just smiled and shook our heads. We knew Daddy would have the last say, but I was kind of astonished that Edward didn't offer to take care of my meal. Oh, well, maybe he's saving for a wedding gift.

We left the restaurant and went back to the hotel. "Let's go to karaoke," Mama suggested. They had it on Saturday nights, so we all agreed and went to the lounge area. Mama and Daddy sang "Proud Mary." They were all into stage play. The lounge not only had microphones with stands, they had a spotlight too; I guess to give that real perform-ance feeling to the different acts. While they were singing, I asked Edward if he knew about Lamar and Sammi. He looked at me and said, "Touch your nose, touch your nose." I knew that meant yes.

I heard the D.J. say, "Next on our list is Sammi and Tamara, singing 'Weak'." Sammi got up and beckoned for me to come, so I got up and we went to the stage. Sammi and I always liked to perform together in front of an audience, so we thought we were the real SWV group. We finished singing and were ready to sign autographs. "Next up," said the D.J., is "Edward and Lamar." I was anxious to hear what they were going to be singing, but the D.J. didn't announce it like he did for us. I'm sure they told him not to. They get on my nerves always trying to outshine somebody. The music started and I knew the song, but I couldn't think of the name of it. Then Edward started singing, "Put on your red dress…" Sammi and I both busted out laughing, but as I was listening and looking at him under that spotlight looking good, I started wondering if I had a red dress I could go and put on.

It started getting late, and Mama ruined my night by

saying, "We're going to church in the morning, I asked around and Bethel Baptist Institutional Church has a 10:00 a.m. service." Everyone else seemed to be cool with it, because they all just kinda agreed with her. I was thinking, "Didn't I tell them I wasn't going to church when I got grown?" I guess since everybody else is sanctified Edward and I will go so we don't have to hear about it later. As we all walked off the elevator to our room I was wondering, "Is Lamar and Sammi going to share a room now? So, what are the sleeping arrangements now?" I asked kind of abruptly. Daddy looked at me with a solemn look on his face and said, "The same as they were. Sammi and Lamar will handle their business when they get back home." I thought, "Child boo Daddy, they already been handling business." Then I thought how I had been judging them for days not knowing the whole story. I couldn't help but think how Mama use to always say, "Judge not, or you gone be judged…Matt. 7:1." I felt bad.

Mama and Daddy stood there watching us like kids, so we exchanged kisses, and walked in the room ahead of them. "Goodnight ladies," said Mama, and we said goodnight and went to our room.

I looked at Sammi and said, "I could kill you for not telling me, but since you got my little niece inside of you I guess I will let you live." She smiled and went in the restroom. I yelled, "Hurry up so we can talk!" When Sammi came out of the restroom, and I looked at her and asked her why she didn't talk to me about all of this. Again, she explained that she didn't want to upset me, or make me feel like I made the wrong decision by not eloping when Edward asked. I guess I understand it all, but I still think that as her best friend I would have told her. After talking for about an hour, she asked me, "So what do you want to know?" She knew that I wanted her to let me know if she was a virgin when she got married, and how her first experience was; however, I didn't want to make her uncomfortable. I said, "Nothing, I'm happy you're my sister."

Sammi knew me too well, she stared at me and said, "Yes, I was a virgin when Lamar and I got married, so save your body for your husband. It's a breathtaking, cherished experience." I just sat there smiling, glad to hear her answer. She then said, "That is another reason we gave our lives to Christ. We want to be obedient and we want Him to bless this baby. It's not enough to just think you are a good person. No one is good and there is nothing that dwells in us that is good. We need the Holy Spirit to make it. I thought I was good because I had not had sex yet, but the Bible teaches different." I looked at her with a disturbed look on my face, "Sammi you sound like my Mama." Then she asked me if I had considered giving my life to Christ. "Girl my mama gave my life to Christ! I'm going to bed." She laughed and said, "That's not how it works T." "Goodnight Sammi."

CHAPTER ELEVEN

Born Again

I was awakened this morning at 5:00 a.m. to the same words, but a different voice. Sammi was saying, "This is the day that the Lord has made, let us rejoice and be glad in it." OMG!!! Then I heard Mama say, "Time to meet with Jesus." I know they are about to drive me crazy now. Everybody a holy roller now. They gone put Edward and me under hell! I was okay with going to church, but now I don't even want to go. Everyone gathered and we prayed as usual and we had breakfast. Sammi and Mama cooked again, and I talked to Edward, dismayed because he would be leaving in a few hours.

After breakfast, everyone went to get dressed for church, then met downstairs in the lobby. Of course, I was the last to arrive, and everyone had a unit on their face when I got there. So, I said very sarcastically, "Praise ye the Lord Saints." We all walked to the vehicles. Sammi and Lamar rode with Edward and me. I wished they had ridden with Mama and Daddy so I could vent to him about Sammi turning into Mama. I guess we should have asked for one of their cd's because when Edward cranked up the car,

Eminem, "I'm Having a Relapse" was playing. Edward rushed and changed the station to the local radio channel that was playing Christian music. A song was playing called "Praise on the Inside" by J. Moss. I knew Lamar was going to start singing; he always liked J. Moss music, but what surprised me was that Edward started to sing too. Not that it bothered me, but I didn't know that Edward knew many church songs. I mean I had never heard him listen to church music before, and he never shared with me anything about Christian music. Interesting! Very interesting!

So, I was glad we had finally made it to the church because everybody in the car with me was acting like they were about to shout. I was thinking about what Sammi was talking to me about last night, and I wondered if Lamar had been talking to Edward about giving his life to Christ also. We parked and went inside. Service didn't start until 10:30; I guess Mama wanted to make sure we made it on time. I would hate to think that she was lying. The pastor's name was Bishop Rudolph something, and he preached about not waiting too late to get things right with God…or something like that. When he did the altar call, my heart dropped, because Edward stood up and started walking towards the front. What in the world is going on? If Edward gave his life to Christ before we got married, then I would have to keep going to church. Wow! I feel like God has a sense of humor now. I said I was not going to church once I got out my parents' house, and now the man that I'm about to marry is acting all churchy. I started to pray, "Lord…" then I stopped myself. What was I going to pray? So, Mama and Sammi both held my hand, one on each side of me. I didn't know why they were holding my hands; I wasn't going up there. I watched as my fiancé accepted Jesus Christ as his Lord and Savior. Now where do we go from here? I know I've heard Mama talk about saved people and unsaved people can't be together.

Edward walked back to the pew where we were sitting and gave me a hug. Then he gave Mama a hug, and gave Lamar dap. All I could think was, "Ain't this something." My family was thrilled about what had just happened, and now I guess I could either join them, or be the outcast. The service ended, and I did not give my life to Christ. I couldn't do it just because Edward had done it; I had to have my own relationship with God. I had to do it for me and not for Mama, Daddy, Sammi, Lamar or even Edward. Mama looked at me as we walked out the church and said, "Don't wait until it's too late." We got in the vehicles and Lamar called Mama on her cell phone and asked, "Where y'all want to go and eat?" They hung up and Lamar said, "KFC it is." Typical church folk always wanting chicken after church on Sunday. I was kind of speechless. Edward held my hand; I guess he knew that I was a little overwhelmed with what had just happened. I seriously was concerned about the future of our relationship now.

We pulled into KFC, and I already knew what the conversation was going to be about once we all sat down to eat. I dreaded going in and sitting for what would seem like forever with them all, and my attitude showed it. Mama said, "You don't have to be mad at us. We aren't going to preach right now." I wanted to roll my eyes, but my Mama did not play. I didn't want her to slap me, especially in front of Edward. We ordered and sat down to eat. As expected, Daddy started the conversation, "Edward, I'm really proud of you.

We should get together so we can go over some important things a newly converted Christian needs to know." Edward nodded his head and told Daddy, "Yes sir." When will he sit down and talk to me about this? There is absolutely nothing wrong with him giving his life to Christ, and I know that God is needed in a marriage; however, I thought we could have some fun once we got married before we did the Jesus thing.

After leaving KFC, we went back to the hotel and Edward and Lamar prepared to leave. We were sitting in Edward and Lamar's room and Sammi went into the room with Lamar, to have their goodbyes. So, I suggested that we walk across the hall to give them some privacy and so Daddy could talk to Edward about converting, or being born again. We walked into their suite and they were in the bedroom, being a husband and wife also. I thought to myself, all these sanctified freaks; who does this in the middle of the day, right after eating? I said, "Let's go down to the pool." I wanted Edward to hold me, but now he all holy and I wasn't trying to tempt him, but I felt lonely.

Edward saw the distress on my face and grabbed my hands and looked me in my eyes and said, "Tamara, I love you. We're going to be okay." I blurted out, "How are we going to be okay? I don't want to give my life to Christ just because you did. Are we even supposed to get married now? Our wedding is in a few weeks Edward; you should have talked to me about this." He looked me in my eyes, put his hands on my shoulders, and said very firmly, "No I should not have talked to you first, my relationship with God is mine, and I'm not walking away from you; however, to be the best husband I can be to you I need the Lord."

I could not even argue with him; I knew he was right. My mama had been teaching me stuff a long time. I knew for a fact that my parents had the best marriage that I knew of, and I'm sure Lamar remembered that too. Him getting married and accepting Jesus reflected our parents having a relationship with the Lord. I knew that I needed to give my life to Christ. I was feeling some type of way.

As we walked around the pool deck I asked, "What are you doing so important that you have to leave today?" He told me that he had to go to a meeting for the Arizona Classic Jazz Festival which was November 6-9. Then he said, "Babe, August 23, is the Charlie Parker Jazz Festival in New York. Do you want to go?" I thought about it for a while, and then replied, "Um no, I don't and neither do you. That's our rehearsal dinner night." He explained that he would be flying up early that morning, and back in time for the dinner. I asked in an agitated voice, "Edward, what if something goes wrong and you don't make it back in time?" So, he replied, "God will make sure I'm here." This dude! Now he's been saved ten minutes…I looked at him and said, "Praise ye the Lord." I wanted to make sure he knew all the different dates for our wedding events, so I gave him an itinerary with them listed. "Babe, put these dates in your phone: August 11th, we go and get our marriage license. August 15th, is my bridal shower. August 23rd, is our wedding rehearsal & dinner. August 27th, is my bachelorette party. August 29th, the men have to pick up tuxedos, and August 30th, that's our wedding day." I was being facetious with the last date. He looked at me and said, "Don't forget August 22nd, my boy is throwing me a bachelor party!" I kissed him and said, "Yes, he is Brother Edward, so glad ya Born Again!" I was laughing so hard at myself I was in tears.

CHAPTER TWELVE

My Friend Willie

After waking up and praying today, Mama sent me to the truck to get magazines that she wanted me to look at. She wanted me to start on some of the wedding arrangements like, making sure the caterer knew what time to arrive, checking that the dress was coming along, being sure the church was booked, and a lot of other stuff that Mama had already done, she just wanted me to put my hands in it since it was my wedding. So, once we were done with breakfast, I asked Sammi if she would like to help. We went to the computer room at the hotel and printed a calendar for August, so we could write all the dates on it and what we needed to do once we got back to Winterville.

As we were planning, I looked at her and said, "We need to give you a bridal shower." She and Lamar had done everything so secretly, no one did anything for her, or bought her a gift. She said, "No, this month is all about you." I knew she would make a great sister-in-law. She wouldn't let me throw her a shower, but I planned to present her with a gift at my bridal shower. I still told her that I was going to give her the biggest baby shower anyone has ever had. She said I had to wait until after her fifth month. How people gone be superstitious and saved? You either trust God or you don't. It takes too much work to be saved and superstitious. I just said, "Okay." I didn't have time to get into an argument with her about her beliefs.

My phone rang, and I didn't recognize the number but I answered anyway. After I said hello I heard, "Sexy T, what's up?" I smiled, because I knew who it was. It was Willie. "Sexy T, what are you doing tonight? We are having a farewell party on campus, you should come by." There was a moment of silence, and then he said, "It's just an innocent goodbye gathering." I thought about it and told him that I would get back with him later. Sammi asked me what Edward was talking about, I replied, "Excuse me?" She said, "That was Edward, right? All that smiling you were doing." I kind of brushed her off and pulled out the magazines that mama told me to go get out of the truck earlier. Let's get some ideas out of these magazines. There is: Brides, Forever, Wedding, and Bridal Guide.

After noticing the titles, I said laughing, "Girl why your mama-in-law had to buy three of each magazine?" Sammi's eyes lit up as I sorted them across the table, and I knew then that she wished she had a chance to have a wedding. I asked, "Sammi, do you regret not having a wedding?" She looked at me and smiled, "No, I told Lamar that for our fifth-year anniversary we can do the wedding thing. We will have saved money and we can have a nice ceremony, so honestly, no. I am excited about helping you with yours though." I was glad that she was helping me too; Sammi and I have been like sisters for years and I was happy to share this experience with her. We could use the next few days to make sure everything was going per schedule. I thought about Willie's offer to come to the college to tell my graduating class goodbye. I mean, we have been here together like family for four years. I didn't want to go by myself, but I knew for a fact that Sammi wouldn't want to go.

I decided to ask her anyways, "Sammi, my friend called and said he's having a going away gathering on campus tonight. Would you like to go?" She looked at me and said, "We're girls, right?" I nodded my head yes, and then she got deep on me. She and I had always told each other the truth, but she had never done it from the perspective that she did it from this time. She asked, "Is that who called you earlier?" I said, "Yes." Then she finished, "You have a good man: One who loves you, respects you, honors your beliefs, and more importantly one who has given his life to Christ, but you still want to play games. That is usually what happens when little girls get real men. It's time to grow up Tamara, and don't allow the devil to mess up your blessing. The reason I say that is because I saw how you were smiling while talking to *your friend* on the phone…the same way you smile when Edward calls." I tried to jump in and defend myself, "But…" Sammi wasn't having it, and she said unfalteringly, "No buts, we have plenty to do tonight planning your wedding." I guess she told me, I wanted to go off, but she was absolutely correct. I looked at her and said, "I love you friend," and she gave me a hug and said, "I love you too sis."

Daddy was taking a nap, so Mama came out to help us with the wedding planning. Mama knew what she was doing. Mama always talked about being an event planner, but instead, she helped Daddy with the business. She had a binder that had dividers for every single portion of the wedding, and it all looked so organized. My mama was the best and I loved her for everything that she had done for me. She talked to Sammi about eating healthy and exercising. That went on for hours and then Mama made tuna fish sandwiches and sliced mango for lunch. We ate, and I guess Daddy taking a nap was welcoming, because we all decided to take a nap too. Of course, Mama made Daddy a plate and left it in the refrigerator for him. She was such a good wife.

I heard my phone playing, "And I am telling you..." I knew that Edward was on the other end. I noticed myself smiling from ear to ear, just like Sammi had said I always do when it's Edward. He was texting me, "I love you babe. I made it to Stone Mountain and I will be flying out early in the morning to Arizona. I'll call you in the morning after you all pray." He knew beyond a doubt that I would be up early for morning prayer. I replied, "I luv u 2, glad u made it safe." He replied, "To God be the glory." So, I guess he's sho nuf saved now, sounding like my Mama and Daddy. "Goodnight babe." Edward giving his life to Christ was going to take some getting used to. It's not like being around a saved person was abnormal for me; it's been a part of my entire life. I can get with it; it's just not where we were.

Morning came, we prayed, and right at 5:35 a.m. my phone went off. "And I am telling you..." I felt kind of bad because we had just finished praying, kind of felt like I should have changed the ringtone. Oh, well, I answered, "Hey babe." Edward said, "Hey, babe. Is prayer over?" I told him yes and we talked for only a short time. He told me to ask Mama to pray for his flight, and I told him that I had already prayed for his flight. He said, "Great, we're on one accord and you're already submissive." What did he mean by that? I'm submissive; did he think that I'm going to be doing what he says now?

We ate breakfast, got dressed and went shopping to get Mama a dress for the wedding, and of course Daddy stayed at the hotel watching TV and snoozing. We went to what seemed like every store in Jacksonville. We were all over Jacksonville at stores like: *The Bridal Shop, Macy's, Dillard's, David's Bridal,* and *The White Magnolia.* Finally, Mama said, "Let's go back to Dillard's and I'll pick from the two we put on hold there." My response was, "Um, let's go get something to eat first! We have been shopping for hours. I see why Daddy doesn't like to come with us now." Mama said, "We can grab something from the food court." We still ended up going straight back to *Dillard's* first, and then stopped at the *Chick-fil-A* in the food court an hour later.

Even though Mama had put two dresses aside to choose from, it still took her forty-five minutes to decide what she wanted to do. They both were very pretty. One was a Tadashi Venice Lace & Tulle dress which cost $369.00, and the other was a KM Collections Bolero Jacket dress for $220.00. Mama liked them both a lot and she couldn't decide which one to get. Then she did just what I knew she was going to do, she purchased them both. "I can wear one to the wedding and then change for the reception." She's such a diva. I said, "Ma, I'm the bride." She replied promptly, "And I'm the bride's mother. You will always be a reflection of me." I thought to myself, "What if I'm looking awful?" And no sooner than I thought it she added, "As long as you are looking good." My Mama always seemed to be one step ahead of me some kind of way. We laughed and went back to the hotel.

On the ride back, I told Mama I wanted to ask her a question. She expected all my questions to be bizarre, so she looked in the rear-view mirror at Sammi. I told her I didn't mind if Sammi heard it, and she told me to ask away. I told her about the conversation I had with Edward this morning and he told me that I was on one accord and submissive. She just kept nodding her head and saying, "Okay." I knew what being on one accord meant, that we agreed about something, but that submissive mess he said was a bit disturbing. So, I finally asked, "What does being submissive mean?" Mama always liked to talk about the Bible, so I knew she was on cloud nine. She said, "Well tell me what made him say it first of all." I told her that he asked me to tell her to pray for his flight, and I told him that I had already prayed for his flight, and then he said something like, we're on one accord and you're already submissive.

Mama laughed and said, "That's not a bad thing Baby Girl. Let me start from being on one accord." I didn't stop her because even if I said just the submissive part, she was still going to say what she wanted to say. She continued, "Being on one accord means to be of the same mind, having the same love, united in thinking according to Philippians 2:2." Well I guess that was a bit more than I thought it was, so I was eager to hear the rest. "And being submissive has been misinterpreted for so long. The Bible does not teach that a woman's submission is senseless obedience to her husband's every command. Being submissive doesn't mean you keep your mouth close when you want to voice your opinion, because you don't want to start an argument.

There is a way to address every issue. A wife's submission is a profound dedication to her husband. She works to have a unity with him. A woman that cannot submit to her husband cannot be on one accord with him. When you are on one accord with your husband and a submissive wife, your husband doesn't have to ask you to pray for him, because you know to do so. Your husband doesn't have to tell you what he needs, you are unified, you are one, and so you know what he needs and you do him no harm. That woman is made perfectly for her husband to meet and comprehend his needs." Then she said, "That my dears, is a submissive woman, and a godly man appreciates a virtuous woman."

My mama was a virtuous woman. My Daddy always showed Mama he appreciated her. Then I said, sounding like a child asking for a Christmas gift, "I wanna be a virtuous woman Mama." She looked at me, smiled and said, "You will be baby." Then I asked, "Do I gotta go to church to do that? I'm joking, Mama." Sammi was laughing so hard, and when she regained her composure she said, "I'm going to be a virtuous woman," Mama looked at her and said, "You better be."

We arrived back to the hotel, and my phone received a text. "So I guess you aren't coming to the party?" It was Willie. I thought about what Sammi had said earlier to me, and what Mama said in the truck, so I replied "Nope, tell everyone I said goodbye and have a blessed life." When we opened the suite door, Daddy had already started cooking dinner. I could not believe we had been gone for so long. Mama walked in and gave daddy a big hug and a kiss, and he embraced her as if they hadn't seen each other for months.

Yes, it seems that having God in your marriage is a good thing. I texted Edward, "Love you, babe," and he replied, "I love you more."

CHAPTER THIRTEEN

Goodbye Duval County

We did our morning prayer, and Daddy said, "Let's pack up and leave, there's no reason to stay until Wednesday." I guess he was right, I had cleared housing, and Mama had her dresses for the wedding. Sammi quickly said, "Good! I get to see Lamar a day early." We smiled. We were very happy that Sammi was a part of our family, and she knew it.

Once everyone was packed up, we called for the bellhop to come and get our luggage, and we sat and talked until they arrived. "So Sammi, what do you want a baby girl or boy?" Daddy asked Sammi. That was strange because Daddy didn't usually talk about such things, but this was his first grandbaby and he was talking. He said, "I would love to have a grand boy, yep that would be nice." Since I am my daddy's baby girl and he is showing interest in this new grandbaby, I decided right then that I wanted Sammi and Lamar to have a baby boy.

As we pulled out of the parking lot of the Wingate, I thought about how long I had been in Duval County. There were butterflies in my stomach as we were leaving and passing the university. That chapter of my life is now over, and I had to move on to another period in my life. I smiled because I had successfully completed and received my degree, my parents were proud of me, and I knew that I was truly blessed. Goodbye, Duval County!

I talked to Sammi about baby names until she started falling asleep on me. I needed to ask my mama a question, "Mama, are Edward and I unequally yoked?" She looked at Daddy, and then she said, "Go to the Bible app on your phone and search 2 Corinthians 6:14. After you read it, we will talk." Then Mama put in Kurt Carr's cd with "For Every Mountain." Mama loved that song, and we loved to hear her sing it. Nevertheless, I put my earplugs in for my ipod and put on Anthony Hamilton's cd. I opened the Bible app on my smart phone and began to read to myself, from the CEB version. "Don't be tied up as equal partners with people who don't believe. What does righteousness share with that which is outside the Law? What relationship does light have with darkness?" This said to me that Edward and I are okay together. I believe in the same God he believes in. I fell asleep certain that I was correct.

When I woke up Sammi was already awake, and she was reading some book. Mama looked back at me and said, "Well, what is your understanding of 2 Corinthians concerning your question?" I told her, "I feel like Edward and I are both equally yoked, I believe in the same God he believes in." I didn't want to start my mama to preaching, so I had my fingers crossed that I was correct. She looked at me and said, "No sweetie. If you believed in God, you wouldn't have a problem with church. To believe in God is to have full confidence in His Word and know that it is true. The

Bible teaches in Hebrews 10:25 that we should assemble our-selves together. We as believers should meet, together and stimulate one another." I looked at my mama like for real Ma? Just because I don't want to go sit up in church all day on Sunday means I don't believe in God? Like she always does, she read my face and answered, "Tamara, that is some-thing simple, and you want no parts of it." I said, "Mama, I don't mind going to church, but sitting up in church all day is crazy to me. Half the people that come fall asleep because it's so long. Church is not the building, it's in my heart."

Sammi jumped in and said, "Girl when is the last time you've been to church? Other than the service we just went to on Sunday?" I thought about it and I hadn't been to church. Every time I went home to visit for the holidays I made sure to leave early Sunday morning or come Sunday afternoon. I slept in late on Sundays in college; so, I guess the Sunday Edward gave his life to Christ was the first Sun-day in a while. As I thought about it, that service wasn't that long and I really enjoyed it. I know I must go to church when I get to my parents' house, so I may as well get ready to enjoy church.

Mama cleared her throat to get our attention, "As I was saying, Tamara you aren't hot for God or cold, and the Bible teaches in Revelation 3:16 that God wants nothing to do with you because you are lukewarm." I guess Mama was saying that I needed to get on fire for God. Of course, Mama said, "You better get it together before Edward realizes he's hot and you're not." "Mama I plan to get hot, I just don't want to do it for the wrong reasons." So, she said with such solemnity, "Any reason is a good reason to surrender your life to God."

I thought about what she was saying. I wanted to be on one accord with Edward. I wanted us to have a blessed marriage like Mama and Daddy. Mama then said, "Both you ladies should go to the women's conference with me. It's this Friday and Saturday." Neither Sammi nor I replied. Then Mama said, "You can both let me know tomorrow morning, and I will buy your tickets when we go to Bible Study tomorrow night."

I was so deep in thought about giving my life to Christ that I hadn't noticed that we were home. Daddy pulled up into the driveway, and I just smiled. It had been a long ride, and although it was still early in the evening, I was tired. Tomorrow was a new day and time to prepare for another milestone in my life.

CHAPTER FOURTEEN

Change Of Plans

Although my life seemed to be moving rapidly, being home was reassuring. I was glad that I had a few weeks to share with my parents in the home I grew up in before getting married and moving with my new husband to Stone Mountain, Georgia.

During prayer, I had been thinking a lot about my relationship with God or the lack thereof. I was coming to an understanding that just because I grew up in a house with parents who were saved, and kept me at church all the time didn't make me saved. Christ was not in me, and I knew that I needed to have my own personal relationship with God. Neither my mama, my Daddy, nor my soon to be husband could do it for me. I had to accept the Lord as my personal Savior for myself. Mama was talking to me about a two-day women's conference on tonight and Saturday night. I am hoping the conference gives me the courage to surrender my life.

Three days had passed and I hadn't talked to Sammi since our ride from Duval County on Tuesday. She and

Lamar were busy getting their new apartment in order, and she was trying to do it all before she went back to work on Monday. She called earlier to say that she would be coming over a little later. I asked her if they needed any help, but she said they were pretty much done. I told her that when she got here that she could help me and mama with wedding plans. Mama and I were making sure things were going according to her wedding schedule. She was making calls and setting up meetings for everything. I was supposed to be helping, but Mama had taken over. I was day dreaming about Edward and becoming a woman of God.

I was thinking about what we could do when he came in a few days. He was still in Arizona, but would be returning to Stone Mountain on Saturday night. Then he would be coming here late Sunday evening. We had an appointment Monday morning at the court house to get our marriage license, something we should have done a month ago, but he was always so busy with his job. Edward would only be here for one day, but I was hoping we could get some quality time in.

Mama said, "Girl what's on your mind?" I replied, "Mama, Edward works a lot. Do you think he thinks I'm just going to sit at home while he's busy working all the time?" Mama said, "You all should have had your counseling at least a month before your wedding. You all getting counseling three days before the wedding is crazy to me." I asked, "Why do you say that Mama?" She replied, "Because you seem to have your own agenda and that is not what marriage is about. You two will become one once you are married. You will work together to be on one accord."

After getting situated in my new role as a wife and in our new home, I would embark on finding a career. I had already planned to find a job once I got to Stone Mountain, and I had been looking at several positions with Delta Airlines in Atlanta. I had not mentioned any of this to Edward, but I guess I should have. I wanted to be a good wife, but it seemed so hard. Mama made being a good wife look easy, and she always credited God for that. That was another reason I needed my own relationship with God. Giving my life to Christ was constantly on my mind, and there was absolutely no reason I shouldn't.

Just as I thought about salvation my phone rang, and it was Edward. I answered, "Hey babe, how are you?" He said, "I'm blessed, how are you my love?" He seemed different since he gave his life to Christ. He talked differently, and I don't mean in a bad way. It was just something different about him, and I was happy that I was about to marry this man. I replied, "I am doing well, just waiting on Sammi so we can plan out some things. What time will you be here Sunday?" The doorbell rang and I yelled, "Mama, Sammi is at the door! Can you get it please?" I continued my conversation with Edward, "Babe I have really been thinking that I want to give my life to Christ." His reply was, "So what is stopping you?" I told him that I was planning on going to church Sunday and doing it, and then I asked him "So how is Arizona?" He said, "Perfect, we had our meeting on Monday, and the manager there is so organized that all I had to really do was look over and sign off on some papers." I interrupted, "So you're done?" He said, "Yes I am…"

Then there was a knock at my bedroom door. I uttered hastily, "Come in Sammi, its open." I wanted to hear what

Edwards plans were for the next two days, so I beckoned for her to come in without even looking so I could hear him clearly. I said, "Hello, Hello? This negro done hung up on me!" I turned around to tell Sammi, and Edward was standing in my bedroom. I heard the doorbell rang again, it was Sammi that time, but I could care less.

I screamed with enthusiasm, and gave Edward a big hug and a kiss. I couldn't help but wonder where in the world is my daddy, because he would not allow Edward up to my bedroom. I don't care how close we were to being married. Then I heard Mama say, "Okay, y'all bring this downstairs before your daddy realizes what's going on." I was kind of surprised that Mama allowed him to come up, but she was standing five feet away so Edward couldn't even grab my booty if he wanted to. Edward hadn't been around me that much since he gave his life to Christ, but the short time we were together he didn't touch me like he had before. He gave me a holy hug and holy kiss, but nothing too daring or sinful.

We walked downstairs, and Sammi was sitting on the sofa. Edward asked me, "So why would you wait to give your life to Christ when you know it's what you need to do?" I waved at Sammi and then I answered Edward, "Because, the doors of the church will be open and that's when people do it." He smiled and said, "No baby, we can do that right now." He called for my mama, "Mrs. Daniels, can you come here please?" I was looking at him bizarre and said, "What are you calling her for?" Mama came and Edward said, "Tamara wants to give her life to Christ." Mama said, "Praise God, Honey can you come in the den please?" I couldn't understand why they all were freaking out. Then Daddy walked in and Mama told him what was going on. Sammi chimed in with Mama, praising God, and then Daddy said, "Praise God." They all acted as if I was an evil spirited little witch.

"Okay, am I that bad?" I asked. Daddy said, "Yes you are, if you don't have Christ as the head of your life." It was silent for about ten seconds, and then Edward said, "Tamara, you know how this works. Open the Bible to Romans 10:9-10." Then he handed me the big King James Version family Bible that always sat on the center table. I opened it to the chapter and verse that he told me and read, "That if thou shalt confess with thy mouth the Lord Jesus, and shalt believe in thine heart that God hath raised him from the dead, thou shalt be saved. For with the heart man believeth unto righteousness and with the mouth confession is made unto salvation." Edward was correct, I knew that scripture.

So, then I just began to pray: "Father in Heaven, I come to you in the name of Jesus. I confess that I am a sinner, and I am sorry for my sins and ask that you forgive me. I believe that Jesus Christ, Your Son died for my sins, and I turn from my wicked ways. God, Your Word that I just read in Romans says, if I confess the Lord my God and believe in my heart that God raised Jesus from the dead, I shall be saved. So right now, I confess Jesus as the Lord of my soul, I accept Jesus as my own personal Savior, and as of right now I am saved. I thank you Jesus for dying for me, and giving me the opportunity to have eternal life. Amen." I had heard Mama lead people to Christ many times with this prayer.

Once I was done, my mama grabbed me and gave me a

hug. She was crying with tears running down her face. Daddy said, "Congratulations Sweetie, now study that Bible and get you some power." I looked at Edward and the first thing that came to my mind was a song I heard Shirley Murdock sing called "Usher Me." My man had just ushered me into the presence of the Lord. I felt so blessed and this was a feeling I had never felt in my life, and it felt good. Sammi nudged me and said, "We are double sisters now, sisters in Christ and sisters-in-law." Daddy was rubbing off on her, because that was corny.

I wanted to know what Daddy meant when he said, "Get you some power," so I was ready to start reading the Bible, and unexpectedly eager to go to the women's conference Mama had bought tickets for Sammi and I to attend with her tonight and tomorrow. I asked my daddy, "Where do I find the power at in the Bible Daddy?" He said, "Start with the four gospels, Matthew, Mark, Luke, and John. Then ask the Holy Spirit to lead you from there." I gave Edward a hug, and was shocked when he said, "Praise God, now we can still get married," then he laughed. I did not find the humor in that. Was he gone just leave me at the altar?

CHAPTER FIFTEEN

Beautiful Evening

Edward, Lamar, and Daddy spent the evening male bonding last night at my parents' house. Sammi, Mama, and I went to the women's conference at Mama's church, Deliverance. I enjoyed myself, and not once did I look at my watch to notice the time. It was a lot of praise and worship, and I could benefit from the minister.

The guest speaker's name was Minister Brenda Y. Smith, and it was kind of funny that the message on last night was, "Being on One Accord with Your Man." The same stuff she was talking about was what Mama had talked to me about earlier this week. I was digging the way she explained it using Matthew 18:19 (ESV): "Again I say to you, if two of you agree on earth about anything they ask, it will be done for them by my Father in Heaven." She said, "Have you ever seen a couple that was so in love that it almost made you sick?" At first I was like, saved people aren't supposed to be jealous and then she said, "Repent right now for being jealous. That is what happens when husband and wife agree together, and then go to the Father together." Minister Smith had some good points. I could see my mama and daddy as that couple she was talking about.

Sammi seemed to be enjoying herself last night too. I am praying that she and I can help one another through this journey together. I'm so glad that I gave my life to Christ and that I have such a wonderful group of people to help me. Sammi, Lamar, Edward, and I are all new babes in Christ, so maybe we can grow together and become the strong powerful saints that my parents are.

Tonight, is the dinner at the conference and each woman gets to bring her man. It's a formal event, and I am excited that we get to triple date. I never thought I would want to go out with my parents, or my brother. I am anxious to hear what the message will be about tonight. Minister Smith was so real and to the point. I recall her saying last night, "Now, those of you, who are married, go home and be on one accord with your husband. Y'all that ain't married- go to bed alone."

That meant Sammi and Mama could go home and get their freak on. I, on the other hand, was going to bed alone, and that is just what I did. Edward was sleeping over at Lamar and Sammi's apartment, so he and I talked on the phone for a little while, and he reminded me that we would be married in twenty-one days. I asked him if he had a nice suit for the dinner, and he assured me that he had all of that under control. I already knew he did because he did not cut corners when it came to dressing. I had to make sure I had something nice to look as good as he was going to be looking.

Going to purchase something was out of the question. The wedding was only three weeks away, and I didn't want to ask my parents for money for anything because they were already doing so much. That is one reason I didn't say anything about a graduation gift. I had plenty of dresses that I could select from to look dazzling next to Edward, and not to mention my fabulous shoe collection. Lamar always joked with me about my shoes. He called them stripper shoes, but I didn't care. I loved me a nice pair of stilettos.

The day went by and it was time to get ready to go to the conference dinner. My mama suggested that the men get ready at Lamar and Sammi's place and that the ladies get ready at my parents' home. She said, "We can make it like a prom night, and the men have to come and pick us up too." I looked at my mama and said, "Who fixing to be playing games?" She laughed and said, "It will be fun, you will see." So that is what we did. While we were getting ready, it was kind of fun laughing with Sammi and Mama about the guys. I said, "Mama why you wanted to split up this way to get ready?" She looked at me and said, "Role play is fun in a marriage." Then she walked in the bathroom to take her shower. I looked at Sammi and said, "She is really a freak." Sammi laughed and said, "Your daddy's."

I was finishing up my hair and the doorbell rang. I walked to the door, and before I could open it Mama said, "Wait!" I looked at Mama in amazement. Mama had on a red and white pants suit. The pants were red in the back and white in the front, and the jacket she had on was white with red buttons. Her jacket stopped right pass her butt, and her shoes were white with a red 4" heel. She had on diamond earrings that dangled, and her hair was cute and cut as always. Mama picked up the phone and dialed a number. I could hear the phone ranging on the other side of the door. Then she said, "Honey, we are going in the den. Count to twenty and then you all come in."

I guess Daddy said okay, because we went into the den and stood there. I thought, "Daddy played games too?" Wow! Sammi was cute also. She had on a black loose fitting spaghetti strap gown with a shear scarf across her shoulders. Her hair was up in a bun, and she had on silver earrings and shoes.

I had on a strapless glittering gold gown that hugged my body, but not too tight. Mama would have had a fit. The shoes I had on were gold open toe 5" heels with stones on the heel. Mama let me wear her pearl necklace and earrings. My hair was pinned up with a few curls dangling down my back. I looked like royalty.

When the twenty seconds was up I heard the door open, and we stood there in anticipation of what we would see. First, Daddy came around the corner. My daddy had on a white suit, with a long jacket, a red tie, and red Stacy Adams shoes. He had a red and white corsage in his hand for Mama. He gave it to her and gave her a kiss. My parents looked remarkable. They looked like that couple that was made to be together. I looked at them and said, "Wow!"

Then Lamar stepped in, and he had on a silver suit, white shirt, a black and silver tie, and a pair of black Stacy Adams shoes with streaks of silver in them. My brother gave his new bride a red rose and a hug; they were cute. I was excited to see Edward, but I was nervous too. I was fidgeting with my dress, and Mama said, "Stand still, you look fine." My chocolate truffle came around the corner with a black and gold pinstriped suit on, a black shirt, gold vest and gold bow tie. His shoes were Elation, and they were black with a gold tip at the toe. He handed me a single white rose.

I smiled at him and he said, "I love you, babe." He took my hand, lifted it and twirled me around and said, "You look like a queen." Daddy said, "You all look beautiful."

Mama had to have told the guys the different colors we were wearing because we were all color coordinated. Daddy said, "Let's go." None of the guys had keys in their hands, so I wasn't sure who was driving. I thought that maybe they all drove so no one would have to get into a back seat. We walked outside and were astonished to see a white stretch limo in front of the house. Mama looked at Daddy and said, "Good job honey." So, they were into this role play stuff. I felt like it was prom night.

Sammi and I were simply amazed. I was hoping that Edward was learning from my daddy how to woo his woman. He's good right now, but I want to make sure I'm wooed when I get old as Mama. We all got into the limo and there were wine glasses and a bottle in the ice bucket. Daddy said, "Let's have a drink and toast to good looking black folks." Daddy pulled out the bottle of Welch's grape juice. I thought to myself, "Are we having communion?" My daddy was tripping. I hoped he didn't try this at my wedding.

We got to the church, and I noticed Daddy's truck, Edward's car, and Lamar's car over in the far left of the parking lot. I was laughing because my daddy must have told them at some point that he wasn't paying for the limo to sit while we were inside. Daddy was not wasteful with his money. The limo pulled us over to the church's banquet hall. The men got out when the driver opened the door, and Daddy gave him a $20.00 bill. Then daddy helped Mama out, Lamar helped Sammi out, and Edward helped me out of the limo.

We walked into the banquet hall onto a red carpet, that was beautifully decorated. The color pattern was red and gold. I should have known that Mama and Daddy's attire was corresponding to the theme. The lights were dim, and candles were everywhere. The tables had authentic red and gold rose petals on a red table cloth. The centerpiece on each table was a clear vase with red and gold marbles inside, and a dozen red roses. I don't know who decorated, but it was breathtaking.

The usher walked us to our table, and the men pulled out the seats for us to be seated. After I sat down, Edward bent down and kissed me on the cheek and said, "I love you." I was blushing, and my heart felt so joyful. I was looking around like a little girl in amazement of everything. "I didn't know saved people did it like this," were my thoughts. There was a live band playing slow instrumental music, and it sounded like love music. Couples were dancing together, and everyone just seemed happy.

The emcee stood and said, "Welcome everyone to Deliverance's 2008 Annual Women's Conference Dinner Gala. We have a full itinerary for tonight, so without further ado we will get started." Then she read the entire agenda and said, "You will not hear from me again until it is time to bless the dinner, so if you are scheduled to minister pay attention to your program, and get on up when it's your time." After she said that, a young lady walked to the front. Everyone clapped as she prepared to minister with a praise dance. When the music started, it was Shirley Murdock's "Usher

Me." That was so amazing to me that I had just thought about that song when I gave my life to Christ, and now she was dancing to it. As my heart was touched to the lyrics, the music, and the dance, I decided that I had to change the music I had selected for my wedding. I had to have "Usher Me" in my wedding.

The night went on and then a lady stood to do a poem. The title of her poem was "Just to Be His Queen." When she first started the poem, I thought she was talking about her man, but towards the end I realized she was talking about being a queen in the Kingdom of God. It was indeed a beautiful evening. After the emcee stood again and blessed the meal, the instrumental music was playing and couples were dancing again. Daddy stood and walked over to me and looked at Edward and said, "I'm going to dance with my baby if that is okay with you." Edward smiled and said, "May I dance with your wife?" Daddy said, "No sir," and then he smiled and nodded his head yes and gave Edward the okay.

Once the servers started bringing plates close to our table, we left the dance floor and went to wash our hands before partaking in the meal. The food looked good. It was chicken, yellow rice, green beans, and hot rolls. I wanted a salad, and to my surprise there was no salad. They did have lemonade and tea. It was a typical dinner menu, but it was good. They served red velvet cake for dessert.

While we were eating dessert, the minister from last night stood and said, "I want to thank you all for coming out, and you all look marvelous. Remember to continue to love one another, don't take one another for granted, and thank God for one another. Have a blessed night, and thanks again."

The emcee stood and said, "I want to invite you to Deliverance for morning worship tomorrow at 10:00 a.m. If you do not have a church home, we would love to have you and you will be a blessing to us."

The evening had come to an end and it was time to leave. We all walked out, and I had forgotten that the limo wasn't going to be there. We all separated, and I walked to the car with Edward. Lamar yelled to Edward, "Hey man, you got a key, right?" Edward said, "Yes," and then he opened the door for me, and I got in. When he walked around to the other side of the car and got in, I knew he was going to tell me he loved me, but I wanted to say it first. So as soon as he sat down I said, "I love you, babe and thank you so much for this evening." He looked at me and said, "I just want to make you happy." Dear God thank you for this fine man.

Edward took me straight to my parents' house, and they were pulling into the garage as we pulled up behind them. He asked me if I wanted him to come in. Of course, I always wanted him with me. I asked, "Are you sleepy?" He said, "No." I replied, "Then yes, you can come in for a little while." We went in and sat in the den. We talked about church tomorrow, wedding plans, and our honeymoon. After talking about that for a while, Edward said, "I'm going to leave now. We shouldn't discuss the honeymoon again until wedding day." I agreed with him, gave him a kiss and he left. God had blessed me, even before I realized it.

CHAPTER SIXTEEN

Sunday Morning Worship

We did our normal prayer this morning, and I asked Mama and Daddy if I could lead prayer. They both agreed that I could, so I did. I enjoyed praying with my parents. It made me feel as if we were on one accord. After I prayed, I asked my daddy if people that were not married could be on one accord. He grabbed his Bible, and said, "Act 1:13-16 tells how the disciples were on one accord with Mary in prayer and supplication. So no, you don't have to be married. You just should desire the same thing, and serve the same God.

After prayer, we ate breakfast and begin getting ready for morning worship. My phone rang, "And I am telling you..." I needed to change my ring tone. I answered, "Hey babe," because I knew who it was. He asked, "Are you getting ready for church?" I told him yes I was and that I was almost done and ready to go. He asked me if I wanted him to come and get me or if I was riding with my parents. I said, "You know I want to see you, babe. But, if you need to finish getting ready we can just wait and meet up at church."

He then said something and I didn't know if I was pleased he said it or troubled by it. He said, "The Lord must have delivered you from your selfish spirit right away." Then he laughed. He thought that I was selfish? He must have. Why would he say that if he didn't? I said, "Okay, well I'll see you at the church babe." I kind of had an attitude. I didn't think I was selfish. He's never called me selfish before, and now that he's so holy I was selfish.

"Mama!" I yelled for my mama so I could ask her. She said, "Yes Baby." I asked, "Do you think that I am selfish?" She said, "You have your moments," as she was putting on her shoes. What did she mean by that? "Daddy," I had to ask my dad to see what he thought. "Yes Baby Girl." I asked, "Do you think that I am selfish?" Daddy said, "No, I think you are spoiled." That was fine with me and that's all I needed to hear. I already knew I was spoiled.

We left and arrived at Deliverance. I saw Edward still sitting in his car. I decided that I was going to be mature, and not act like a spoiled brat. Clearly Edward didn't know the difference between spoiled and selfish. Daddy parked next to Edward, and everyone got out the vehicles. I didn't see Lamar's car anywhere, so I wasn't sure if they would be here or not. I didn't need them to be at church, but I wanted Sammi to go to the mall with me after church. I guess I would just call her later.

Edward told my parents good morning, and then he walked towards me and said, "You know I love you, right?" I looked at him and said, "I know babe, let's go and be ministered to." We walked into the church, and sat down. It was only 9:45, so there was fifteen minutes before church started. Mama was passing out wedding invitation reminders. My mama was so efficient, and I loved her for all the planning and support she was giving us.

I forgot that my Bridal Shower was on Friday, August 15th, until I took one of the reminders and read it. The way Mama had them designed had the wedding reminder to the right and the Bridal Shower invitation to the left. Yes, my mama was the best and I just had to thank God for blessing me with her.

When Edward looked at the announcement he said, "You get a Bridal Shower and a Bachelorette party?" I said, "That's just how it works." He said, "That's how it all starts. The women get everything." I grinned and since he brought that up I asked, "Are we supposed to give each other a wedding gift?" He looked at me and said, "You are my gift, babe." Edward always knew just what to say to make me blush like a teenage girl. I'm not sure if I should be blushing about that, especially in the Lord's house, but he always made me smile.

I started thinking of how Edward reminded me of my daddy. Daddy was so in love with Mama, and he said things to her constantly as if he was flirting trying to gain her attention. Mama always blushed, and said, "God, I love this man." Sometimes she would say it aloud, and sometimes she would say it in a mumble, but she always thanked God for Daddy. She would always tell me, "Your daddy is a Godly man, there's a difference in a Godly man and a good man. You see, a bad man can pretend to be good for only so long, but a Godly man is good forever. He looks so good loving on God, that even when he makes you mad you still love him." I guess having a Godly man is certainly something to be thankful for, and that's why I was so thankful for my Godly man.

Service was about to start, so we hushed up for the welcome. The little girl went to the microphone, and said, "Greetings Saints." I remembered when that was my job on Sunday mornings. "Welcome to Deliverance morning worship service, and feel free to receive your blessing in Jesus name." I felt kind of old watching her, and reminisced on the many years I spent in Deliverance doing many things. Our parents kept us busy in church business. Lamar and I sang in the choir, we ushered, and we participated in every church activity that was going on.

I understood it all now that I had accepted the Lord as my personal Savior. The older I got, the wiser my parents seemed to me. They were training us up in the way we should go. Even though I said I wasn't going to church when I became an adult, because my parents had done what the Word of God had told them to do, it was inescapable. God's Word declares that it will not return to Him void. They had instilled Godly principals in us, and now, Lamar and I both were children of God.

I noticed Sammi and Lamar walking in the side door. My brother hated being late, so I know it had to be Sammi. Whenever we went somewhere together, Sammi was always late. I could tell by the look on Lamar's face that he was upset about their tardiness. They walked over to where we were, and Sammi had that church finger up in the air. The one that makes people disappear and not be seen when they moved around in a church service. That always made me laugh, because that finger would go up and the person would always kind of hunch down about a half inch. I can only imagine what a six-foot man or three-hundred-pound woman huddling down was supposed to do. Oh, well, it seemed to be church protocol, so I did it every time I went out during a service.

After the little girl that did the welcome sat down, the choir stood to do praise and worship. Even though the little girl brought back memories of my childhood, Deliverance wasn't the same. I was expecting to hear lined hymns from the amen corner and the deacon board, but the first song was Kirk Franklin's "Melodies from Heaven." I was standing, clapping, and rocking from side to side. The choir sounded good, and to my surprise the musicians did too. After they finished that song I sat down and thought, "This is fun."

The choir went right into another song. It wasn't as up-beat. It was Smokie Norful's "I Need You Now." The rendition from the choir was exquisite, but what touched my heart was to see Edward worshiping and praising God. I don't think he has ever looked better to me. Oh, my goodness, now I see why my mama said a Godly man looks good loving on God. I was thinking that even an ugly man would look good if he was praising God. I laughed inside, and shook my head. Something was wrong with me. Why did I have such thoughts in the middle of that lovely worship service?

Once the praise and worship was over, it was time for offering. I didn't attempt to open my purse because I knew I didn't have one cent. My daddy noticed and he handed me a five-dollar bill. I thought that was so funny because that's just what he did when I was a little girl when it was offering time, and then Edward handed me another five. I opened my purse to put the five in that Edward gave me and he asked, "What are you doing?" I whispered, "I'm going to put in the money my daddy gave me," and I put the five dollars Edward gave me in my purse.

Edward was giggling, and then the person that speaks while you're getting out your money so you don't skimp God said, "Will a man rob God?" Edward leaned in to me and softly said, "No, but Tamara will." I started laughing and pulled out the five dollars. When the offering plate came to our pew, I put both five dollar bills inside. Edward said, "Awe, you gave from your heart." Had I known he was going to be the offering police I would have sat by my mama.

After the offering, the Pastor stood to feed us the Word of God. I was excited to receive the Word. The Pastor said a few jokes, which I thought were very funny and then he said, "I won't be before you long today." That must be written down in the preaching rules somewhere. Every time I have ever been to church it's been said before the preaching starts.

The subject of his message was, *"Don't Give up on Your Dreams."* He talked about believing in your God given talents, and that God wants His people to be blessed. He also talked about not being discouraged because it seemed people who didn't serve God were successful. We should seek Him first and His righteousness and the desires of our heart will be fulfilled. His message reminded me of a blog I used to follow by Woman Highly Favored of God, called: *"Going after this Gift from God."* That lady was straight to the point, and so real. In fact, the minister that ministered at the conference we had just gone to kind of reminded me of that lady from the blog as well. I like messages I can understand.

After service, we lingered for a while at the church chatting, and then we headed to my parents' house for some of Mama's good soul food. My mama cooked every Sunday, and the family got together and had quality time. We played cards, video games, board games, karaoke, swam, basketball, and of course my daddy had a weekly scripture that he read and explained to everyone. That was his chance to witness to all my cousins, Auntie Carolyn, Auntie Nikki, and Uncle James, my mama's two sisters and brother. They didn't live in Winterville, but they lived close enough to visit every Sunday because that's how good Mama's food was.

Family was important to Mama, and even though no one ever brought a covered dish or anything, Mama never complained. She was happy to see her sisters and brother every week, and she always made sure she had containers for them to take an extra plate home with them. I enjoyed my cousins, and I was glad Edward could see how close my family was. It did tick me off weekly that none of those greedy negros offered to help clean, because I ended up doing it. Sammi offered to help, so I was glad she was a part of the family now.

Sammi and I loaded the dish washer, and she said, "Tamara, remember our dreams to become singers?" I looked at her and recalled the message from today's service, and wondered where she was going. I said, "Yes." She said, "I think we can do it, if we put the effort into it."

I looked at her and said, "So you want me to write gospel songs now?" She replied, "Yes, you can do it through Christ Jesus, and He will bless the works of your hands." I continued to clean as I thought about the idea. I love to write, but I had never written any gospel songs. Maybe I could do it, but I would be leaving with my husband in a few weeks, and Sammi is about to have a baby soon.

I told her we would discuss it later. I wanted to pray about it first and talk to Edward about it. I envisioned her and me receiving an award at the BET Gospel Awards, and as soon as I thought about that I heard my mama's voice saying, "Only what you do for Christ will last." Just like the pastor said this morning, God wants us blessed, but we must seek Him first.

Our family continued to play games and socialize until early evening, and then people started fading away. Good-byes were said, and by 7:00 p.m. it was just Mama, Daddy, Edward, and me. We sat down to watch a movie together. Mama had Tyler Perry's collection of movies, she loved his movies. So, she picked *"Why Did I Get Married?"* Now I'm about to get married in two weeks and my mama picks that movie for me and my fiancé to watch. Wow!

Edward left about 9:30 p.m. We didn't have too much to say about the movie after it was over. He was looking at me kind of strange because I was so hyped by the scene when Shelia played by Jill Scott knocked her husband Mike played by Richard Jones across his head with a wine bottle. He was rude and disrespectful to her and I felt like that's what he deserved. I didn't dare start a conversation about it for my mama to get started.

CHAPTER SEVENTEEN

Court House Revelation

Edward called me this morning at 4:45 talking about he couldn't sleep. Man, I had fifteen minutes left to sleep before my mama started her morning rituals and he had to take that away. I said, "What's wrong babe?" He said, "I think we should get some exercise in today." Was he trying to tell me something? I didn't make a big deal about it. Instead I just asked him, "What time would you like to go?" He said, "We can go right after we go do the marriage license thing." So, I guess that is how we will be hanging out today. I felt like something else was bothering him, but it was too early. I decided that I would try to figure it out later. As soon as I said, "Okay babe, I'll see you in a few hours," Mama was at my door. I just sat straight up and took a deep breath.

After our morning prayer, the doorbell rang. Who could that be? It was only 6:00 in the morning. I opened the door and it was Lamar. I asked, "Where's your key loser?" He didn't answer my question. He just asked where Daddy was at and kept it moving. Mama was in the kitchen cooking breakfast and Daddy was sitting at the table reading his morning paper. I kept walking, so I don't know what they discussed. I was so tired I didn't even feel like being nosey. I was concentrating on getting back in my bed until it was time to get up and get ready for Edward to come and pick me up.

Mama woke me back up at 7:45 and told me I needed to come and eat. So, I got up, went and took a shower, got dressed, and went down for breakfast. Daddy and Lamar were still sitting at the table. Now that I wasn't so sleepy anymore, I wondered what they had been talking about for so long. They both had empty plates in front of them, and some papers that I couldn't tell what they were, but I did see Clean Shine Janitorial Products logo at the top. He needed to hurry up. He and Sammi were to be our witnesses at the courthouse today.

They didn't seem too concerned, so I guess it wasn't that serious. I made my plate, and sat down at the table to eat. I wanted to ask what was going on, but my daddy didn't like it when people asked questions concerning his business. I would have to get the news from Sammi later. I was sure that Lamar would share with her, so I just sat there quietly.

There was a knock on the door, and I knew that was Edward. Mama said, "I'll get it." I heard her making a commotion about something, and I heard her say, "This is so sweet." I wondered what she was talking about, and then Edward came in the kitchen with an Edible Arrangements bouquet in his hands. I looked at him and smiled. God, I love this man. I did try to figure out where he got it from so early in the morning. Then I thought about what Mama said at the spa in Jacksonville, "Stop trying to analyze everything." I said, "Thank you babe," and he said, "I love you babe, and you don't have to ever worry about knocking me out with a wine bottle."

I burst out laughing as he greeted Lamar and Daddy. He then looked at me and said, "Let's go." I grabbed my gym bag so we could run the lake once we were done, and he being the man that he was, took the bag from me. Edward looked at Lamar and said, "Don't be late." Lamar said, "Yes, ten, right?" Edward replied, "Yes," and we left.

Mama yelled, "I'll put this fruit in the refrigerator after I eat a few berries." Now I didn't want her to open my arrangement, and I thought that she was joking, but if I had made a fuss about it Lamar would have opened it for sure and took a big chunk out of it. So, I didn't say a word.

We got to the courthouse parking lot, and Edward cut off the car and took my hand and said, "This is it. You're going to be my love forever now." I looked at him and said, "Jesus, you, and me." I was very happy with my life. I was excited that I had given my life to Christ, had finished college, and was about to get married to the most wonderful man on Earth. Lamar and Sammi walked in as we were being called, and I was glad they did because Edward had begun pacing the floor.

As we finished signing all the papers and made the payment for the marriage license, I was a bit surprised that the lady said, "Congratulations, Mr. & Mrs. Wilcox." I said, "In a few weeks." She said, "Well the wedding is really just a ceremonial event to celebrate with family and friends." Edward kneeled and gave me a kiss. My thoughts were everywhere, and I assumed Edward was thinking the same way I was.

SANCTIFIED FREAK

Lamar and Sammi told us they had to go to work so they left. As we were getting in the car I thought, "The most romantic thing would be if Edward had reserved us a room so that we could do what married folk do." Yes, we had made it, and I was a virgin when I got married. I said to Edward, "So we're married now." He smiled at me and I said, "Exactly what kind of exercise did you have in mind."

He said, "We can go to the community center and play some one on one basketball." I replied, "Basketball! We're married now, Edward." He looked at me and I winked at him. He said, "What are you saying Tamara?" Now if I had to spell it out for him maybe he didn't want me. I knew I was ready to break him off, and I could not understand why he was not thinking like I was. I said, "Nevermind," and I had an attitude. My whole demeanor had changed. I thought, "We've been married ten minutes and already he done pissed me off."

We got in the car, and I sat there pouting like a child. Edward looked at me and said, "Talk!" Oh, he wants to make demands now that we're "married." I said, "Edward we have been waiting to get married so we can have sex, and all you can think about is basketball." I thought I was going to cry my eyes out after he said, "First, we aren't going to start things off with you getting an attitude and shutting down. If you're feeling a certain kind of way, we need to talk about it. Now, Tamara I haven't been waiting to marry you so I can have sex. You are so much more valuable to me than just sex.

Of course, I want to make love to you, but that's not why I wanted to marry you. You are my help meet, the one that

108

will help me in all affairs of life. We are going to have our wedding in a few weeks. Your dream was to walk down the aisle as a virgin, and I want that for you. I don't want to just have sex today, and leave you tomorrow to go back to Stone Mountain. I want us to see this thing through until the end. I'm in this for the long-haul Tamara. I have the rest of my life to make love to you," and then he wiped the tears from my face and kissed me, and said, "I love you, babe. Now, let's go so I can beat you on the courts."

Oh, my goodness, I felt so blessed that God had blessed me with this man, and I also felt so bad because I probably made him feel like I was some kind of crazed horny jezebel. As Edward was driving to the community center, I wanted him to know that I wasn't a scarlet, so I stuttered trying to speak, "I...I... am glad we're waiting until the ceremony, I mean whenever it happens it will be special." He said, "Oh girl don't be saying no whenever it happens, August 30th is coming soon and I'm just as excited as you are. I am not trying to hang around at no reception all night long. I am going to be ready to take my bride home, and not see the outside until time to go to Italy for our honeymoon."

We made it to the center, and played a few games of one on one. I don't know why he wanted me to see him all glistening, and looking so sexy, but we had a good time. I asked him why he felt like we needed to exercise today. He said, "Because my tux is a little tight, and I refuse to have to move to the next size up." I laughed, but it made me think about my dress. I hadn't tried it on since I had been back. I needed to talk to Mama about it when I got home.

After we left the center, Edward asked me if I was hungry. I was sure that Mama had prepared lunch so I told him I was, but we could eat at the house. He said, "Your Mama is amazing, glad you have her DNA." Now I didn't say anything, but Edward already knew that I couldn't cook. I looked at him and said, "She sure is." On the ride home, I had decided that I wanted to ask Mama to give me cooking lessons for the next two weeks. Maybe I could learn to cook something before we got married, or should I say before our wedding ceremony because that negro was already mine.

CHAPTER EIGHTEEN

Plans, Plans, Plans

Once Edward left the house last night, I started reflecting on our conversation. Edward was a good man, and I knew I needed to work on some things. I was simply spoiled, and I knew it. As many times as I had said that I wanted to be like Mama and Daddy, and talk things out with my husband, but the first thing I did when I got mad was shut down. The more I thought about it, the more ashamed I was of myself. I just started to pray. "Dear God, I know that I need to grow up, and be a strong woman, a help meet to my husband, and the Godly woman you have called me to be. God forgive me for being ignorant. Lord I need your Holy Spirit to lead and guide me as I transform into a mature spiritual woman. Amen."

I felt renewed after my prayer as if I had learned a lesson about being that nagging wife Sammi talked to me about in Jacksonville. I was astonished during prayer this morning, because Mama prayed for me to become a virtuous woman, and be a passionate and wise wife. I told Mama about my prayer, and how I thought it was so neat that she kind of prayed the same thing for me. She said, "Baby, God sends confirmation of His word." I knew what confirmation meant, but I didn't understand her statement. She must have seen the perplexity on my face. After a few minutes, she said, "2 Corinthians 13:1 says: 'By the mouth of two or three witnesses every word shall be established'."

I still did not understand what Mama was talking about, but I didn't say anything because I knew she wasn't done talking yet. She continued by telling me that God sends confirmation of His Word with signs and wonders, through preaching and teaching. She told me that I should seek God daily, and expect confirmation. I wondered how my mama got so smart. She always had good advice, and I couldn't think of her ever telling me anything wrong.

My phone rang, it was Edward. He and I talked only for a short moment because he was getting ready to head back to Stone Mountain, and he didn't like talking on the phone and driving. He said, "Babe I'm in countdown mode now. It's August 12, 2008. In eighteen days, we will become man and wife to the world. I am so happy that I found you, and I promise you that I'm going to love you like Christ loves the church." I was blushing and smiling so hard my face was hurting.

I told him to drive safely and call me when he arrived in Stone Mountain. As soon as we hung up the phone, I was already missing him. I guess it showed on my face, so Mama suggested we go to the store and get the needs for the Bridal Shower. She was more excited about this entire event than I was. I was honestly only excited about one thing, and that was getting to Stone Mountain with my husband so we could do what married folk do. It wasn't all I wanted, but all this other stuff that had to take place now was irrelevant to me.

As I sat and thought about things, long engagements were stupid to me. I had never had sex before, and I was aroused. So why would people get engaged for a year or years before getting married? It seemed like a set up from the Devil if you asked me. I knew I wanted Edward more and more with every kiss. I was glad that he wasn't staying around for long term, because my body was wanting him bad. The closer we got to our wedding date, the more I wanted to experience him as my husband.

Mama asked, "You ready Baby Girl?" I grabbed my purse and said, "Yes ma'am." Mama of course had a three-ring binder labeled "Tamara's Wedding," with a divider for each event of the wedding. Under the "Bridal Shower" divider was a list of things to do for the shower on Friday. The theme of the shower was "The Marriage Heel." Mama knew I loved heels, so that is where she got that idea from. Mama told Daddy we would be back soon, Daddy said, "Yeah right! I'll be gone to play golf. Have fun, and don't spend too much money." Mama laughed, and said, "Yeah right."

Mama looked in her planner and said, "Okay, first to "Ideal Bride." That was a store with all kinds of party favors for brides to be, and anniversary things also. We pulled up in the parking lot and the building was made like a big wedding cake. We walked inside and everything one would need for an elegant event was in themed sections. Mama said, "This is the way we need to go," as she walked up the stairs of the very luxurious looking building.

Once we made it up the stairs, my eyes lit up when I saw

the section that Mama was headed towards. It was everything made into heels. There were: heel balloons, heel goodie bags, heel candy dishes, heel plates, heel centerpieces, and everything one could think of. I wondered how we would carry everything we needed, but once we got to the area a young lady said, "My name is Tia, and I will be helping you today with all your shopping needs." She had on a cute dress, and 5" stilettos.

I looked around to the other themed areas, and noticed that there were personal assistants in every area dressed to oblige the theme. The bowling themed area lady had on bowling shoes and a bowling t-shirt, and the lady in the magician themed area had on a black cape and black top hat. The entire store was cute. I still didn't think that she would be able to help us with everything, but that didn't stop Mama from starting her order.

Mama said, "I know this is a dumb question, but what colors do you want for your shower?" I said, "Purple, and you know it Ma." Mama told me a while ago that I needed to think outside the box, and be creative. My wedding colors were purple and gold, so I thought the bridal shower should follow suit. So, Mama said, "Okay, purple it is. This is your day."

Mama looked at the lady and said, "We need centerpieces for eleven tables, three balloons for each centerpiece. I want one round metallic gold balloon, and the other two heels purple and white…" Mama was a woman that knew what she wanted. I admired her boldness and confidence as I listened to her make demands in a very respectful way. I wanted that. Yes, my mama was the inspiration I needed to be a successful woman, and I appreciated her for it.

Mama purchased plates, cups, and napkins all with a heel design. She also purchased goodie bags designed like a heel, and all kinds of goodies to go inside of the bags. I was getting excited about the bridal shower. I wasn't sure what the difference was between the bridal shower and the bachelorette party, but I did not complain. I loved the attention.

Once we left *"Ideal Bride"* Mama looked at her binder and said, "Now, to the venue and caterers." I asked, "Are they the same?" She said, "Yes, the place is called *The Elite*. I knew the place. I didn't tell Mama because Sammie and I had snuck to a party that our friend Gilda was having. We didn't know it was a "Chippendales" party. That's when I should have given my life to God because I thought we were going to die in that place. Half-naked men were everywhere, getting all up-close and too personal for me. Undeniably, it was not a place for two young girls.

Once we arrived to *The Elite*, I acted as if I had never seen the place before. We walked in and were greeted by a handsome, bright complexion young man. He was about 6-feet tall, had a broad build, jet black wavy hair, and hazel eyes. Oh, my goodness this brother's eyes were gorgeous. "Good afternoon ladies. My name is Thomas; how may I serve you today?" Mama said, "We have a reservation for Friday, and Ms. Diane said that we could come in and do a floor plan for tables and sample the menu." The very attractive young man nodded and said, "Yes, let me grab my notebook, let the chef know that you are here, and we can do that right now."

As we waited for him to return, Mama said, "The chandeliers are exquisite this would have been a beautiful place to have the reception after the wedding." Before I could respond, Thomas was walking back towards us with his notebook in hand. "Okay ladies, you can tell me exactly how you want things set up, and if you wish I can offer suggestions that I think will fit your needs.

So, we looked and Mama surprised me. I thought for sure she was going to take control again like she did in Ideal Bride, but she looked at me and said, "Tell him what you want." A little speechless at first, I stuttered as I began to speak. "I...I...," then I pretended I was my Mama, and stood tall and began to speak. "I would like a small table upfront for me with the heel centerpiece and heel balloons in center. I don't mind how the other tables are set up, as long as there are ten round tables that seat eight people each, and a table for gifts and a cake table."

Thomas said, "Very well, you can both sit here and the chef will bring out two main entrées for you to choose from for your event." I was hungry, so I was ready to sample anything to curb my appetite until we went for lunch. All that planning was hard work and I was tired of the whole process. Not only was I ready for it to be over with because it was so many details, I was ready to go be with my man.

The chef finally came with two entrées: Chicken Marsala, and Beef Tips on separate plates. He also sat two plates with a single serving of egg noodles, green bean almondine, and a dinner roll on them. Those would be the sides no matter which entrée we picked. After he placed them on the table he said, "Once you are done, I will bring out the dessert choices." Mama said, "Thank you," and we began to eat.

They both were delicious to me. Mama asked, "What do

you think?" I knew she would have the final say, I just felt like she was trying to make me decide. I kept chewing, put my finger up, and closed my eyes to suggest that I was making up my mind. Then after about fifteen seconds I said, "Let's do both." I waited for Mama to shut that thought down, and she said, "Good idea, some people may prefer one over the other." You would think that I just made and executive decision. I was so excited that she approved my suggestion.

Thomas and the chef walked back in and asked if we were ready to sample the desserts. I was mad the chef was trying to take my plate before I had finished. He asked, "Are you done?" I looked at Mama's plate and she still had a little portion left, but she shook her head to give the approval to take the plates. I remembered her telling me before, "A lady never scrapes her plate." So as bad as I craved to keep my plate to finish every single piece of food, I reluctantly sat back and pushed the plate away. I wanted to ask her, "Is that in the Bible."

The chef signaled for the kitchen staff to bring in coffee and three different desserts that mama and I had to choose from. There was: Red Velvet cake, Strawberry Cheesecake, and German Chocolate cake. I knew I didn't want the German Chocolate cake, but it did look appealing. The other two looked divine, and I couldn't wait to eat them both.

Mama was always so sophisticated about things. I guess she could tell I was about to dive right in, so she looked at me and said, "We will TASTE them all, and then decide," putting emphasis on taste. She also handed me a different fork than the one I had eaten the meal with, and said, "Use this one." At this point, I was just doing what Mama was doing to make sure I didn't embarrass her.

First, the staff placed a slice of the Red Velvet cake in front of both of us. While we tasted, they began to pour our coffee. As I watched, I noticed Mama took a sip of coffee after tasting a small piece of the cake, and that is what I did also. Then she pushed it in front of her. I wanted to say, "Now wait a minute. I ain't done yet." However, I followed Mama's lead and pushed my plate forward.

The staff then placed a slice of the German Chocolate cake in front of Mama and me, and again Mama tasted a small piece of the cake, and then she took a sip of coffee. I didn't like German Chocolate cake, but I took a small piece, and to my surprise, it was amazingly heavenly. It melted in my mouth. I had my eyes closed, and for some reason I started thinking about kissing Edward. It made me excited about us becoming one.

Mama said, "Baby Girl you must really like this one, your eyes all rolled back." I opened my eyes, and took a sip of my coffee. I said, "Oh, yes this is good. I didn't think I would like the chocolate." I was kind of embarrassed, because my thoughts about Edward had taken me to another place. I pushed the plate to the side and asked, "Can we please try the next dessert now?"

The chef nodded, and placed a slice of the Strawberry Cheesecake in front of us. He also added more hot coffee in our cups as we each sampled the cheesecake. Mama said, "Oh my goodness, this is delicious." I still had chocolate Edward on my mind. She looked at me and said, "What do you think?" "It's good, but the other two were better," was all I said. I was still trying to figure out why the cake made me think of Edward.

"Well, we have to make a decision," was her response, and then she pulled the Red Velvet cake back to try another sample. So again, I happily followed Mama's lead and grabbed my Red Velvet cake. "Give us some time please," Mama said looking at the chef and Thomas. "Yes ma'am," Thomas replied, and turned to walk away. The chef and the other staff followed.

We finished the Red Velvet cake, and then pulled the German Chocolate cake in front of us to try again. As soon as I took one bite, the thoughts of Edward rushed my mind again. I was so glad that the lady told me at the court house that we were already married, because if she hadn't I would have felt like a freak. I had thoughts of us sharing cake together. "Tamara?" Mama interrupted my thoughts. I said, "Let's do the Red Velvet."

Then Mama said something that made me feel like she knew all my thoughts, "You don't think you can handle eating it and staying at the reception without sneaking up to a room huh?" "Mama what are you talking about? You're about three degrees nastier than I need you to be talking to me." She was correct, but I wasn't going there with my mama. She was unquestionably a sanctified freak.

Mama called for Thomas to come back in and told him our decision, and the chef came with big bags on his arms and said, "As a token of our appreciation for selecting us to service your event, we would like to give you the remainder of your meal with all three desserts. We know that you are busy planning, so we hope this will benefit you and ease some of the stress." Mama said, "Thank you so much." They finished some final paperwork and we left.

CHAPTER NINETEEN

Nosey Me

It was 5:15 a.m. and Mama hadn't come to wake me up yet. We had a pretty full day yesterday, but that wasn't like her. I got out of bed and went to my parents' bedroom. I knocked on the door and called, "Mama? Daddy? Can I come in?" Daddy opened the door and I walked in. "Good morning, Mama are you okay?" I asked because she was still in bed. She said, "I have a horrible headache sweetie." I said, "How are we going to pray if you're not feeling well." She looked at me and said, "You pray this morning for us baby." My mama never missed a beat. While she was down, she was still teaching me. I know Daddy could have prayed, but she was showing me that I had the same power to reach God that she had.

I prayed, gave Mama a kiss, and asked, "Do you want me to cook breakfast too?" Daddy said, "No Baby Girl, I'll cook," and he hurried out the room to the kitchen. I was glad. Mama smirked a little, and I walked out the room, but before I closed the door I heard Mama say, "Good job baby, I love you." I replied, "I love you too Mama," and I closed the door behind me. I went into the kitchen and asked my dad if I could help him with anything. He said, "Yes, you can beat a few eggs so I can soft scramble them for your mother."

I thought it was so nice that Daddy cooked for Mama. I knew men did it all the time now, but normally in our house, it was Mama doing all the cooking. I thought that Daddy stepping in to help while she wasn't feeling well was pure love. I helped Daddy cook until I heard my phone ringing, and I knew it was my man. I said, "Alright Daddy, you're on your own Edward is calling." He giggled and kept getting things right for Mama. He was preparing her a nice spread too: grits, eggs, bacon, toast and coffee. I yelled, "Save me some."

I jumped across the bed and grabbed my phone off the night table and answered, "Hello." I heard music playing in the background. It was a song that I had heard on the Jamie Foxx sitcom, "Well it's been five years, can't hold back my tears, 'cause I'm just so happy, I'm marrying an angel today…" I was smiling with tears welling up in my eyes because I had told Edward I wanted that song in our wedding, but I couldn't find it. The music faded. "Good morning My Angel," Edward said in a deep baritone voice. Oh, this man just makes me love him more and more.

"Hey babe.", I said in a shy girly voice, and asked, "Where did you find the song?" He replied confidently, "Didn't I tell you not to worry I would find it?" I laughed and told him that I missed and loved him so much. He chuckled and asked, "What are you doing?" I said, "Cooking breakfast for Mama, she doesn't feel well." He replied, "No for real." He already knew I did not cook. We chatted for a while and then he had to go to work. He was all excited about his upcoming trip to New York.

I didn't know what I would be doing today, especially since Mama was not feeling well. The bridal shop called and said I needed to come and try on my dress. I didn't want to do it alone, but I guess I had no choice. I thought that maybe I would call Sammi and see if she wanted to go with me. We hadn't hung out much, and she was always working. It would be just like old times, and we could talk about that music thing she brought up after church the other day while we were cleaning the kitchen.

I went back in the kitchen with Daddy, and he was taking Mama her breakfast in bed. "I'll take it Daddy," he looked at me, snickered, and said, "You going to pretend that you cooked it?" I took the tray from him, winked my eye and walked into their bedroom. "Mama I have your breakfast," I whispered quietly making sure I didn't make her head throb from loud noises. She turned over, sat up, looked at the food and said, "Right." I'm going to surprise everybody and learn how to cook something. I gave her a kiss and left to go and call Sammi.

"Hello." Sammi answered. "Hey girl, what's up?" I said. Then before she could answer I continued, "You should call in today, and go with me to try on my wedding dress. I'm sure you need some alterations since you got that little bump now for your bridesmaid dress." Sammi said, "Girl, Lamar is not about to let me take off for the whole day." Oh, my goodness, you mean to tell me wives gotta ask their husbands if they can call in too? "So what you're saying is that before you can call out at work you have to make sure you ask Lamar first? Y'all are killing me with this submissive wife stuff. I just don't know."

Sammi was laughing, but I was serious. Then she said, "Girl, stop tripping. I'm working at Clean Shine with Lamar now, and I have to make sure he doesn't need me in order to take off." Okay, so she married my brother and didn't tell me, now she working at my family's business and didn't tell me. I had better pray before I open my mouth because I'm about to go off. I responded nice, "Well, when did all of this take place?" She said, "I just started Monday after we came to the courthouse to witness you and Edward's marriage license signing. I thought you knew. Lamar came to your parents early that morning to ask your father about it."

So, that's what Daddy and Lamar was talking about at the table Monday morning. "No I didn't know, but nobody seems to think I need to know anything. I'll talk to you later." I just hung up the phone. I was mad, because it seemed like they kept leaving me out. I went to talk to Mama about it, but she was resting and I didn't want to bother her. "Daddy," I whined as I walked around the house like a toddler looking for my daddy.

He was in the den. He glanced at me, and then back at the T.V. He was watching Matlock, so I knew he wasn't going to be listening to me. "Yes dear," he said when a commercial came on. Then I pled my case, "Daddy why didn't anybody tell me Sammi was working with Lamar at Clean Shine?" Although I was Daddy's girl, he was always to the point and made it short and crystal clear. He replied, "You aren't paying her, so there was no need." Just as he said that the commercials were ending and Matlock was coming back on.

I sat there mad as heck, but I didn't say a word. After sitting with Daddy for a while, I stood up to walk out. "Wait a minute, little girl." Daddy grabbed my hand and stopped me, but he didn't finish speaking until Matlock went into commercial again. "Listen, you are a young lady now. Everybody business isn't your business. You don't have to know everything. So, before you get all bent out of shape about something that is not your business at all, think about it. You're going to stay mad, especially if you think my business is yours." He let my hand go right as the commercial ended, and started watching Matlock again.

Did he just call me nosey? I think he did. As I was walking out I looked back at him, and said "I love you, Daddy." He winked and continued watching Matlock. Daddy was right, but I wanted someone to understand how I was feeling, so I called Edward. He didn't answer, but I knew he would call me right back. I put my phone close to me while I was getting dressed so I could answer, and just as I was putting on my shoes it rang. I answered, "Hey babe."

"Hey, you okay?" he replied. Then I started my whining, "Babe, Sammi is working with Lamar at Clean Shine." I waited for him to respond, but he didn't. I said, "Hello." Then he responded, "Is there more to that?" I said, "Not really, but I just didn't know." He asked me, "Why would you need to?" I could see already that I didn't want to talk to him any more about this, but before I could say something he continued speaking, "Tamara, you have a wedding to plan, packing to do, and a whole bunch of other stuff you need to take care of. Stop stressing about other people affairs." I asked him, "Are you calling me nosey?" He replied with haste, "You already know you're nosey, I love you, babe but I gotta go." I told him to have a good day and we hung up the phone. I guessed my being inquisitive made some feel that I was a little meddlesome.

I heard the doorbell rang as I was grabbing my purse to head to the bridal dress shop. I opened the door and it was Sammi. She greeted me, "Hey girly, I'm here for you." I was happy that she had come, so I smiled and said, "Thanks girl, you're always here for me when I need you." We got in the car and headed to the dress shop. I noticed she did have a little belly bump, so this was undoubtedly a good thing for her as well. I couldn't help it I had to ask, "So how do you like working with your husband?" Nosey me.

CHAPTER TWENTY

Undefiled Bed

The next day Mama was feeling better. It was 5:00 a.m. and she was as loud and holy as ever. I got up, washed up, and went into the den to pray. We did our morning prayer as always, and after that, Mama started cooking breakfast. "Tamara, did everyone make it to the bridal shop for dress fittings?" Mama asked. I told her yes, and I went and got back in my bed. I was thinking hard about Edward. I was missing him and each day seemed to get worse. I guess it was because we were on countdown until the wedding day, and I wished he was with me.

I decided to read the Bible to get my mind off these feelings I was having. I just picked it up and turned to Song of Solomon, it was like reading a love story. It was very romantic and it made me think I should read another book. The feelings weren't leaving, and I was feeling kind of bad for having them while I was reading the Bible. Just as I had that thought I remember Mama saying, "Marriage is honorable in all, and the bed undefiled." I wondered if that meant ALL kinds of things in the bed. Surely I'm going to hell for thinking like this while reading the Bible.

That was some stuff I wanted to talk to my mama about, but she'll get too deep and gross me out with way too much information. I'll talk to Sammi and see what she tells me. She's saved, married, and I won't get as disgusted by her information. At least I didn't think I would, although she was married to my brother and I didn't want to hear her talk about him either, but I would rather take my chances with her. I needed to know some things before my wedding day.

I went in the kitchen to eat breakfast, and Mama and Daddy weren't in there. Mama had left me a plate in the microwave, but everything else was all cleaned up and they were nowhere in sight. I looked in the den, and then I reluctantly walked to their bedroom door. The door wasn't closed, so I figured it was safe. I pushed it open and they weren't there either. Now I was beginning to get alarmed, because I didn't see them. So, I called for them, "Mama, Daddy, where are ya'll?" I walked out to the back and they were laying together on the lawn chairs looking up at the sky. Whew...I'm so glad they weren't doing anything that I didn't want to walk in on. It was romantic how Mama was laying in Daddy's arms on that narrow lawn chair with such assurance that she was safe, because if he had moved quickly she would have been on the ground. I couldn't tell where Mama's legs began, or where Daddy's stopped. They kind of looked like one lying there together.

I started texting Edward. "Hey babe I miss you." Seeing Mama and Daddy just made me wish that I was in Stone Mountain with him, and we could interlock with one another. "I miss you too babe," he replied immediately to my text. "Hey girl, what are you doing today?" Sammi was texting me just as I began to reply to Edward. "Nothing, what's up?" I texted Sammi, and then continued with Edward. "I'm ready to see you." Sammi texted me back that she was on her way over to chill. I wondered how she was gonna have another day off from Clean Shine, but I guess when your husband is the boss you can do that. I replied to them both because I was tired of texting, "Okay, see you soon." I was glad Sammi was coming, now I could talk to her about the many questions on my mind.

About an hour later the doorbell rang, and Mama answered it. I heard a bunch of squeaking downstairs, I figured mama and Sammi were greeting one another. I was sure Mama was trying to feed her something. Mama felt like she was the only woman that ate healthy while pregnant, and she didn't have a problem telling Sammi, "Girl come on in this kitchen and let me cook you something wholesome for that baby." I was glad that I was not going to be living close to her once Edward and I got married and started our family, at least I thought I was going to be glad.

Finally, Sammi came upstairs and into my room. I looked at her and asked, "Has the baby been fed well now?" She laughed and said, "That's your Mama, gotta love her." I asked, "How you get the day off?" She told me that the office air conditioner was broken and the office was too hot for her. Oh, well, now time for me to ask her about the undefiled bed. "Sammi, I want to ask you some serious questions. If you don't feel comfortable answering them I will understand." She nodded her head and said, "Fair enough, shoot."

I opened my mouth, but the words wouldn't come out. I guess I was kind of embarrassed to talk about these things, but if I don't talk to her I will not know. So, I began to speak, "Sammi, once a man and woman is married, the bed is undefiled, right?" She started laughing and said, "I already know where you're going with this, but yes, that is correct." Then I asked, "Will you please tell me what that means?" She began to speak, and then Mama knocked on the door and walked in. "Hey ladies, your father and I are going on a lunch date. I made a salad and some tuna fish if you all get hungry." I said, "Yes ma'am, and she left."

Sammi said, "I'm so surprised she didn't ask what we were talking about." I said, "I'm not, she got Daddy on the mind, and she doesn't let anything come between her and God or her and Daddy." Sammi had a look of amazement on her face. I could tell she was in awe of my parents' relationship just as I was. My phone rang. "Hello, hey babe." It was Edward and he called me to tell me that his parents would be here for the bridal shower. We exchanged I love you with one another and hung up.

In a depressing voice, I said, "Girl, Edward's parents are coming in tomorrow. I don't know how they feel about me. I mean we smile in one another's face, but we haven't really spent a lot of time together." Sammi looked at me and said, "Not today T. Please don't bring out the drama queen." Sammi was starting to tick me off with always calling me a drama queen. I don't think I'm a drama queen. I do get a little passionate about things, but not overly dramatic.

Sammi quickly changed the subject because she knew that I was about to trip, "So back to what you asked me about earlier." Oh, yeah, I did want her to help me understand what undefiled bed meant. She continued to say,

"Well this is just my understanding, so don't quote me. I believe it to mean that marriage is honorable, and that husband and wife should respect their intimacy with one another. I believe if a husband and wife are doing something that is not moral, something that is rude, or something that is reprehensible, the bed is defiled. Did that help?"

It kind of helped, but I wanted her to tell me what was and was not okay for husband and wife in the bed. She knew I wanted more because she asked, "What do you want to know Tamara?" So I boldly asked, "Is it okay for me to put handcuffs on my husband, just for fun?" She looked at me with widened eyes, and for a few seconds I thought that Sammi's eyes were going to pop out of her head. She thought for a while and said, "Marriage is so much more than sex, but both should seek God concerning your sex life. A husband and wife that are in love with one another, in my opinion, don't need any toys; especially something that puts you in bondage." She did make a good point. She continued speaking, "Whatever a husband and wife does with one another, and they both feel respected and not shameful or regretful is okay. This is only how I feel. You should study your Bible, pray, and seek God concerning this. There is a scripture that says something about nothing new under the sun, so I'm sure God will lead you in the right direction if you seek Him. I believe natural love making the way God created it is beautiful."

I was pleased with her answers, and she didn't get too deep. I had to give her a hug and say thanks, "Sammi, thank you. I am proud of how mature you have become. God sure looks good on you." Then she said something very encouraging, "Keep it exciting, and make him love what he has at home." I must say it was reassuring and interesting because I wanted to be the best wife that I could be, and to do that I needed to do it God's way. It seems to all leads back to God. Every time I talk to someone about being a good wife, or being happy, we always seem to end up talking about God.

CHAPTER TWENTY-ONE

Bridal Shower Day

I woke Mama up this morning to pray, and during prayer, I was excited. I was ready for the day to get started because it was my bridal shower day, and all my bridesmaids should be there. I had been back in Winterville for a little over a week, but I hadn't seen any of my wedding party. Edward's parents were coming in town too, so his mother could come to the bridal shower. I guess his dad would hang out with my daddy or something. I was just so hyped to see my girls.

"Tamara, there's a lot that must be taken care of before the bridal shower tonight, so get a move on this morning. No lollygagging around!" Mama shouted up to me from downstairs while she was cooking breakfast. I yelled, "Yes ma'am!" I had already planned to not lollygag around. I had picked out my attire for the shower, and I was taking a hot bubble bath. My phone rang. I knew it was Edward, so I answered and put him on speaker, "Hello babe, how are you?" He answered, "Hey babe, I'm fine. What are you doing?" I told him that I was taking a hot bubble bath. "Wish you were here."

No sooner than I said it I wished I hadn't. I didn't want to think about us being together until it finally happened. However, once one opens their mouth and says something, words can't be taken back. He was quiet for what seemed like forever, and then he said, "Send me a picture." I could not believe my ears. He must have bumped his head somewhere. I pretended I didn't hear him and said, "What did you say babe?" He said, "You heard me."

All kinds of thoughts were racing through my head. I thought about how he had got mad at me before graduation because I wouldn't give in, and then I also thought about what Sammi said about married couples shouldn't be ashamed of what we do for one another. Even though we're technically married I wouldn't want to send him a picture over the phone. To me, that was embarrassing and not something I would be proud of. "Okay I will." We hung up and I took a picture of my big toe, and sent it to him. That was the funniest thing to me, and I was laughing out loud.

I heard a knock on the door, "Tamara, are you about done?" Mama asked. "Yes ma'am. I'm getting out of the tub now." I thought for sure that Edward would be calling or texting me right back. As I was putting on lotion, I looked at myself in the mirror. No wonder he wanted a picture of me. I was pretty fine, if I did say so myself. I thought for a while... nope not going to do it. He only has a few weeks left to wait, and I am going to make sure we both do just that.

Finally, I received a text. I started laughing from thoughts of what he may have said. I read it and he said, "This is a very beautiful toe; thank you, babe. This is why I love you so much. No compromising." Wow! It's like he was testing me. I could hear Mama's voice from when she used to say, "A real man respects a woman that says no, and means it." My mama did know what she was talking about. I was so happy I didn't send a picture of anything that could have made things bad between me and Edward.

I finished getting dressed, did my hair and went downstairs with Mama and Daddy. "Good morning, all dressed and pressed, and ready to impress." "Who do you have to impress Baby Girl?" Daddy always had to be so straight and to the point about things. "Edward's parents will be here today. I am not really worried about his daddy, it's his mother coming that makes me nervous." That was my way of telling my Mama and Daddy on Edward's mom. Daddy said just what I knew he would say, "Well just be who you are, and if she doesn't like it, it's a good thing you aren't marrying her." Then Mama chimed in just like I knew she would, "If she doesn't like it, she can come and see your mama." Mama was rolling her neck and eyes, so I said something that I knew would either calm her down or make her slap me, "You'll pray for her right Mama?" I asked with a childlike voice so she wouldn't get mad. My daddy started laughing, and Mama looked at me from the corner of her eyes, and replied with a nod of her head and said, "Yeah, Imma pray for her."

Mama gave Daddy a kiss and told him that she wasn't sure what time we would be back, but she would bring him back a few movies and something for him and Mr. Wilcox to eat. How does she stay on top of everything? She doesn't miss a beat. Nothing sneaks up on her. Mama was always prepared, or planning to be prepared. I liked that about my mama. She ran her home well, and her husband loved her very much.

As we backed out of the driveway, Mama was talking to herself. "Okay first we will go and get our manicure and pedicures, then we will go and have a massage. After that, to the salon to get our hair done and have our facials." I looked at the clock in the car and it was 8:15 a.m. Why did we have to do all of this? This means I'm going to be with mama all day long. So, I sarcastically said, "This is going to be a long day." Her retort, "Very long." That was it. Either she didn't hear the sarcasm in my voice, or she just simply decided to disregard it. Whichever way, the day was gonna be long.

We arrived at Fresh Tips Nail Salon first. Mama and I walked in and went straight to the massage chairs to put our feet in the hot bubbly water. No sooner than we sat down, there were two ladies standing next to us putting our hands in bowls of polish remover. No one else was in the salon, so I guess that's why we were getting all the attention. I was kind of glad about it because it would speed up the time. I made a comment about the massage chairs, trying to get Mama to realize we didn't need to go get a massage, "Oh, these chairs are so relaxing, hitting in all the right places."

Again, my cynicism didn't faze Mama, because she responded without missing a beat, "Oh yes, getting us ready for our massages." She was so excited about it too, and enjoying herself. I decided that I would be excited about it as well. I just closed my eyes and started to think about Edward. I wondered if married women thought about their husbands as much as I think about Edward. I am sure that it can't be healthy to always be thinking about another person.

"Mama, what are you thinking about?" My plan was to ask her that and then ask her if it was healthy to always think about your man. She said, "Your father, what else?" I then said, "Do you think about Daddy often?" "All day, every day," is what she told me. Then she added, "I think about different things, but he is a part of me. So, the only time I don't think about him is when I'm handling my business in the bathroom." So, I looked at the people doing our manicures and pedicures to see if they heard her. They didn't look at either of us, but they all started talking in Chinese, and laughing. How embarrassing. I looked at Mama, "Really Mama?" She had no remorse for making that statement, because she supported it by saying, "What? They mess too." Wow, my mama was a trip.

We were all done. Mama paid the cashier and we headed to Day Dreams Day Spa to get pampered there as well. I wanted to skip it until I walked in the doors and remembered just how lovely it was. The ambiance there was always so tranquil and serene. The waiting area alone was enough to relax your body and your mind. The concierge at the front desk walked us back to a dim lit room with nuts, coffee, and juice. Then she asked if we would be having wine, coffee, juice, or water. Mama said, "I'll have white wine, and she will have juice."

No wonder Mama wanted to come get a massage. She gets her little drink on when she gets a massage. She looked at me and said, "Don't judge me." I started laughing, because I didn't expect that. I thought she was gonna have a scripture for me. Then she said, "Daddy can't drink, and I don't want to do anything that will be a stumbling block for him. So, once a month I come and get a massage and have me a glass of wine."

"I thought drinking was a sin." She said, "It's not a commandment, and the Bible says that whoever is led astray by wine is not wise. Everyone shouldn't drink, because alcohol could cause one to not be sober minded or watchful as the Bible tells us to be." I was a little confused, it sounded like Mama was pedaling backwards to me. Is it okay to drink or not? Daddy says, "No," but Mama says, "Yes." I guess this is one of those things I must study for myself and learn on my own. There was one thing for sure, Mama said there would not be alcohol at the wedding, because she will not be the cause of anyone stumbling.

We finally went into the back area to get our massages, and the lady that did mine felt like she knew where every knot in my back and neck was located. I dozed off for what I thought was only a few minutes, but the next thing I heard was Mama calling my name, and the ladies giving the massages were nowhere in sight. "Tamara, get up girl. You must have been really tense." I thought to myself, "Yes, I am really anxiousness about the whole thing."

"Mama, I'm kind of nervous about me and Edward's first night together." She said, "God will make it a night you will never forget." Then she grabbed her purse and headed to the front to pay the cashier for our service. "Thank you ladies, it was wonderful as always. Come on Tamara. Time for our facials." I didn't even know where we were going to have facials, but I kept it moving and followed Mama.

She walked to the passenger side of the car and looked at me. "You have your license with you, right?" "Yes ma'am." "You drive. I never drive after my massage; I usually relax for about an hour." We got in, and put on our seatbelts. "Where to Mama?" "Chanel's. You know I don't let anybody else do my hair." I knew that Chanel was doing our hair, but I didn't know Chanel did facials now, so I asked, "When did Chanel start doing facials?" Mama told me that she doesn't, but she has a lady named Meeka in her shop that does them.

I loved going to Chanel's, because she didn't overbook, and we didn't have to be there for more than about three hours. I remember going to other shops in our town and being there for almost eight hours because beauticians overbook. I liked going to salons so I could enjoy the wash, but a bootleg hair dresser was always quicker.

We got to Chanel's right at 11:00 a.m., and it was just as nice as the nail salon. Mama and I were the only ones waiting. Chanel had one paying, preparing to leave and another under the dryer. Mama headed right to the hot seat. The hot seat was what Mama called Chanel's chair. Chanel introduced me to Meeka, and Meeka led me to her chair so she could start my facial. I wasn't too worried about my facial, but I was praying this lady didn't mess up my eyebrows.

It was 1:15 and we were done. We were both looking marvelous. Mama paid for our services and we left. Chanel said, "See you all later tonight at the shower." We waved, and nodded and left. "Mama, I am hungry. Do you have lunch somewhere on your list?" She said, "I sure do." I started smiling, only to be disappointed to hear Mama say,

"It's called IHouse." She thought it was so funny too. We went to Publix, and Mama picked up some things for Daddy and Mr. Wilcox to eat. "Mama, can I get a sub? I'm starving." She just kept walking getting this and that for tonight. I grabbed me one of those prepackaged Cuban sandwiches and put it in the basket. We checked out, and as we were putting things in the car she said, "Oh yeah a movie. Pull the car around to the Red Box once you're done. I have to run and grab your father a few movies, and then we can head home."

I started eating my sandwich that I got from Publix, then I pulled around to the Red Box to pick Mama up, and she was standing right there waiting. We headed home, and I was glad about it because I was tired. My phone started receiving text messages, but I couldn't touch my phone while Mama was in the car. She always made Lamar and I put our phones in the glove box when we got into a car that we were driving. No texting and driving was Mama's number one rule. Lamar had lost his driving privileges several times because someone called and said he was texting and driving, or Mama called to see if he would answer the phone.

Once we made it home, I pulled out my phone so I could see who was texting me. It was Edward letting me know that his parents should be arriving about 4:00. I was tired and sleepy so I did not respond. It was already 2:35, so I helped Mama get everything inside the house and put up and then I went upstairs to take a nap. "Mama, Edward's parents will be here about 4:00, so will you wake me up at 3:45?" I yelled to Mama as I was heading up the stairs.

CHAPTER TWENTY-TWO

After My Nap

I heard knocking on the door, it was Mama waking me up at 3:45 as requested. "Tamara, it's time to wake up. The Wilcoxes should be pulling in shortly." My nap was too short; I wanted more. I got up and jumped in the shower hoping it would wake me and I wouldn't be so cranky when Edward's parents arrived. While I was in the shower I started singing a song that I wrote a few years ago. It reminded me that Sammi had mentioned something to me about us recording some music. She hadn't said anything else about it, and that was a week ago. I guess she wasn't serious, or she was too busy to put it into action. Oh, well, maybe she realized that I would be leaving soon.

I cut off the water to the shower, and heard the doorbell rang. I knew it must be Edward's parents; they seemed to be prompt just like Edward was. I hurried and put on a dress so I could greet them. I knew my mama would entertain them until I made it downstairs, but I didn't know what she would be talking about. Mama was known to kind of get in people's business. She's met the Wilcoxes a few times, but I wasn't sure how she felt about them.

I walked downstairs and everyone was just sitting there watching a local minister on the Christian Network station. My parents loved watching him. I never watched him much myself, but when I did it was pretty insightful. I waited for a commercial before I walked in the room where I could be seen. It seemed like I was standing there forever. Edward's mother was very pretty. She had a cocoa skin tone, her hair was wrapped and dropped on her shoulders, and she had on an outfit I know my mama was eyeing. Mr. Wilcox was handsome, tall, and dark just like Edward.

Finally, a commercial came on. "Hello everyone," I said kind of nervously. Mrs. Wilcox looked at me and smiled so big, "Hey beautiful, I am so happy to see you." Squeezing me so tight I thought she was going to smother me. I hugged her back and said, "I'm glad to see you too, both of you," as I pulled away to hug Mr. Wilcox. He said, "Hello Pre-T," he was corny like Daddy. The few times he saw me he made the same unbelievably corny joke. I thought, "Really dude", and giggled like I always did as if it were funny to me.

Everyone sat back down, and the program was ending. Mrs. Wilcox asked Mama what she needed help with for tonight's event. As Mama started reading through her list of what needed to be done and how she wanted it done, I walked into the other room so I could call Edward to let him know his parents made it safely. He said something that made me think his mother was a trip, "Tamara, remember you are marrying me okay, not my mama." I replied with a puzzled voice, "Okay." Thinking, "Lord, I hope this lady don't make my mama check her."

I went back into the den with everyone else and Mama was getting off the phone with the event coordinator for tonight's shower. She said that everything was going as planned and that we would be leaving around 6:30, just in case she needed to handle some things once we arrived. I knew Mama, and even if everything was perfect she would still have some things to handle.

We had less than two hours to get ready, and walk out of the door. Mama was in the kitchen getting snacks and appetizers ready for Daddy and Mr. Wilcox, "Tamara, show the Wilcoxes to the guest room. If you all need anything just let me know." I smiled and said, "This way," and they followed me. It only took about 15 seconds, but it seemed like a very long walk because I was thinking about Edward telling me I was marrying him and not his mother.

Finally, she broke the silence. "So Tamara, do you plan to get a job once you move to Stone Mountain with my son?" Wow! It's like she was waiting to get me alone and then attack. I made sure I was slow to speak before I responded. Mr. Wilcox just shook his head and walked into the restroom. I looked at her and said, "I plan to discuss it with my husband, and see what we decide." She looked at me as if I had started a war. I then said, "The towels are on the top shelf in the closet. See you soon," and turned around and walked away. Imma tell my mama.

I went upstairs to my room to get dressed. I could not believe Mrs. Wilcox said that to me! She has never been rude to me, and to do it so close to our wedding day. I knew what Edward meant now. She must have said something to him about it before. I just prayed, because I refused to let the Devil use me to get mad about Mrs. Wilcox's pettiness.

I heard my phone vibrating. I ran to grab it hoping it was Edward and I could tell him about his she-devil mother. "Hello," it was Sammi. "Hey girly, are you getting ready for tonight?" I heard this bubbly voice of excitement coming through the phone. I responded with a voice totally opposite, "Yeah, I guess." Hoping she would wonder and ask me what was the matter.

I began to vent, "Girl, how about Edward's mammie asked me if I planned to find a job once I moved to Stone Mountain with her son." Sammi was speechless for about ten seconds, "And what did you tell her?" Getting mad as I thought about it, "I simply said that my husband and I would discuss it together." Sammi laughed, "Girl, I'm so glad your mama is my mother-in-law. It will be okay, just pray. Don't even mention it to Edward. You can't talk about a man's mama, and think he's okay with it." I was wondering if she had been talking about my mama.

"Okay girl, let me hang up and finish getting ready to go. Please be there by 6:40. Mama said we would be leaving here early, and I don't want to be there too long alone with her and Mrs. Wilcox." I hung up with Sammi, and finished getting dressed. I was looking cute. I had on a pair of white sheer dress pants, a gold blouse, and a pair of white pumps with gold heels.

I walked downstairs, and Mama and Mrs. Wilcox were waiting on me in the den. Daddy looked at me and said, "You are as beautiful as your mama." Mama smiled along with me, and she was blushing as hard as I was. Then she looked at me and said, "Let's go." Mama kissed Daddy, and said, "See you tonight handsome. I won't be late, so wait up for me." Then she smirked at him. I promise you she is a freak all the time with him, as old as they are.

Mrs. Wilcox hugged Mr. Wilcox, and gave him a quick peck on the cheek. There was no flirting, just what seemed to be an obligational kiss. Edward was very warm, and passionate; however, his parents didn't seem to display that same affection. So even though my parents were super freaks, I would rather have their relationship, than a cold routine marriage.

I thought about what Mrs. Wilcox had said to me earlier and I thought to myself, "That's why your husband probably doesn't like you." I guess I will do as Sammi said, and let that go, and think positive about my soon to be mother-in-law. I want to have a good relationship with her, and I think that it is important that we get along. I refuse to be one of those wives always in competition with my husband's mother. I know there is something in the Bible about once a man gets married he is to cleave to his wife, and put his mama 'nem behind him. Or something like that. I wanted to ask Mama, but I didn't want to get into all of that with her right then.

We arrived at The Elite, and Mr. Thomas greeted us at the door. There was valet parking, and a red carpet. My mama knew how to put an elegant event together. I was smiling from ear to ear, and we hadn't even walked into the actual ballroom where the shower was to be held. "Thank you Mama, this is nice." Mrs. Wilcox chatted in also, "This really is, I'm so happy for you Tamara."

There was a white sign in book with lavender pages on a table with purple, gold, and white decorations. The pen for the guest to use to sign in was one of those Quill feather ink sets. The feather was purple, the pen was gold, and the ink was black. I wasn't with Mama when she did all of this, and I wasn't sure if she had purchased it herself or if Mr. Thomas had done it. Whose ever idea it was, it was brilliant. I loved it.

I had a big Kool-Aid smile on my face, and I was very happy to be sharing this moment with my mother and Edward's mother. I had decided that I would kill her with kindness. I haven't done anything for her not to like me, or be rude to me. So, I'm gonna love the devil out of her. Edward is her only son, and maybe she feels as if I'm taking him from her. What do mamas want their sons to do? Never get married? Clearly she's married, and her husband is somebody's son and she married him. I was kind of dazed by all of it, but I was not willing to let it mess with my night.

The Elite didn't look at all like it did the night Sammi and I slipped out and came to Gilda's party. It was looking as if royalty was coming. I am my Daddy's princess, so I guess royalty had arrived. I didn't say any of that out loud. I didn't want to put any negative views into Mrs. Wilcox's head about me being a brat. Edward knew I was, and was okay with it, so that was all that mattered.

CHAPTER TWENTY-THREE

The Bridal Shower

Sammi finally walked in at 6:50 p.m. while I was texting with Edward. He asked me about his parents, and all I replied was, "They are a beautiful couple." He texted back, "What does that mean?" I told him it didn't mean anything, and that it was time to get started because some of the guests were arriving. He texted me, "Love you babe, later." I was glad because I didn't want to get into that with him either. By the time we talk again I'm hoping he will have forgotten about the conversation.

"Hey girl, this is so breathtaking." Sammi said as she walked over to me. Once she made it to me she said, "This is amazing, I really love this." I felt bad that she didn't have a bridal shower, but Mama told me that she had a gift for us to give to her tonight. She was rambling on and on about the exquisiteness of the room, so I looked around to take in its beauty. Each table had a purple tablecloth, gold roses, and a clear vase centerpiece with a lit candle inside. Where did they get gold roses? The ceiling was full of purple and gold helium-filled balloons, and I don't know how they did it, but the chandeliers had specks of purple throughout each one. I was very impressed myself. There was also a table with a drink fountain with grape juice flowing. It was spectacular! I said to Sammi, "This is incredible."

I felt a tap on my right shoulder, and I looked back; it was Felicia, Danielle, and Victoria, all the ladies in my bridal party were here. We all hugged and just started conversing. We talked about everything. Sammi knew all of them, but they were not as tight with her as they were with me. Felicia said, "Hey Sammi, I heard through my mother's cousin's niece that you are married to Lamar." Sammi smiled and said, "You have been correctly informed." Felicia then responded, "Congratulations." Victoria then chimed in and said, "I just want to know how you gone be the maid of honor now?" I hadn't even thought about that. Sammi looked at me and asked, "Does it matter?" I replied, "Not at all, especially since my wedding is only fifteen days away." Then Felicia interrupted being as messy and petty as ever, "Plus, Danielle is the matron of honor, and she's been divorced for six months now." We all just looked at her, and shook our heads. We loved her despite her flaws.

"Don't worry about all of that, it's time for my shower to get started." I glanced at Danielle to make sure she was okay, and she winked at me. Danielle was one of the strongest, intelligent, and loving women I knew. She always gave 100% and was such a good friend. I forgot all about her and Keith's divorce, but she tried to make it work.

Keith and Danielle were high school sweethearts. They started dating in tenth grade, and all the way until graduation they were never apart. They got married three weeks after we graduated, had a nice small wedding, and seemed to be happy. They were only married for three and a half years, and they didn't have any children. She had called me numerous times telling me that he had been unfaithful, and that the females would call the house to speak with him pretending to be a bill collector or the doctor's office. She listened in once, and heard more than she wanted to hear. I told her that I thought maybe they were just too young. She told me, "No, it could have worked, but we didn't have the Lord in our relationship. He started clubbing and cheating. Being married is so much more than simply saying I do. I'm convinced now that you can have all the money, the best sex, and a nice house. Without God, it is nothing."

Keith's family was wealthy, and he inherited money when his grandfather died. Keith started a staffing agency while he and Danielle were married, and she ran that company while he went to school full time at the local university. Danielle did online courses for business, and she was all about making Keith happy. She looked okay when I glanced at her, but I still walked over to give her a hug while the other ladies were taking their seats. "I love you Danielle. Are you okay?" She said, "This is your night, we will talk later, just know that I'm straight."

The music started playing, and it was "The Lady, Her Lover, and Lord." Wow! Mama went way back, but I did like that song. A young lady from church was doing a praise dance to the song. It was nice, and I was more convinced that I had to make sure that Edward and I are on one accord with God. We have got to have that three-fold chord to have that harmony. Danielle never thought that she and Keith would be where they are now. I should minister to her before the night is over.

The servers started bringing out the salads soon after the dance was over, and Mama stood up to speak. I wasn't expecting Mama to emcee this event. She obviously couldn't find anyone else to do it were my thoughts. She picked up the microphone, "Good evening ladies, we are here to celebrate with my little princess who will be getting married in two weeks and one day. Yes, I am counting down. Only because she has an amazing man that adores her so much, and her daddy is stressing about his little girl moving off for good. I'm ready for my man to be okay. Okay!!! Let's bless the food…" Oh, my goodness, my mama is a trip. I prayed she didn't say anything too private in front of all these people. The next thing I heard was, amen. I had missed the whole prayer thinking about what Mama would say.

Mama said, "I'm going to take my seat and let the event coordinator take it from here." Thank you, Jesus. She didn't need to have that microphone for another second. Thomas walked out with three other ladies, and took the mic from Mama. "Congratulations Tamara. Ladies we are going to play a few games, your food will be served, and then Tamara will open her gifts. So, our first game is called "I Know Her the Best," and this game is as simple as it sounds."

The ladies that accompanied Thomas passed out purple pens, and purple notepads with a watercolor that said, "Tamara & Edward" diagonally across the page. I was more and more impressed as the night went on. The Elite made things nice, and memorable for me. We played that game and of course the winner was Sammi, and Mama let her know the only reason she won was because she didn't play. Thomas said, "All gifts will be presented after the last game." I felt like that would also be a good time to give Sammi the gift we had for her.

Then Thomas stood and announced the next game, "Okay ladies, our next game is called Toilet Paper Bride, and I'm sure you have all played this before or you have seen it. Every table picks someone to be the bride, each table also gets ten rolls of toilet paper, along with other supplies. Whoever makes the prettiest wedding dress on their bride in ten minutes is the winner. Tamara will be picking the winner." His assistants were already passing out toilet paper, tape, glue sticks, and a bowl with sequins and beads in it. Thomas said, "It looks like everyone has all the materials to begin. On your mark, get set, and go."

The assistants then became the paparazzi, and started taking pictures. They had those disposable cameras, and flashes were coming from everywhere. Some of the ladies that were being the toilet paper brides started posing for snap shots. It was funny. I was walking around looking, and shaking my head in approval and disapproval just to make things more interesting. One group actually started over as I crossed my arms, and put one hand up to my face stroking my chin with my right hand. I started laughing so hard. I then heard Thomas say, "Two-minute warning ladies."

As everyone scrambled to complete their design, I headed back to my seat only to see that Thomas had placed a chair upfront that read, "Judge Bride." So, I walked to the chair, and it was like a director's chair for a movie. There was a clipboard with papers attached, and a purple sharpie. The top paper attached had table one printed at the top, the next page had table two printed across the top, and so on until the last page had table ten printed across the top. I was to write a score on each sheet for each toilet paper bride's dress.

Thomas instructed the brides to come and stand in front of my chair on big purple and gold circles they had placed on the floor numbered one through ten. Thomas and his team were on point. I didn't even notice the circles until he instructed them to come up and stand on them. I thought, "When did they do this?" Oh, well, the toilet paper brides walked up, and stood on their numbers. I wondered how they knew which number they were, so I looked at the table across from me and noticed that it had a gold balloon with a #1 on it. I then realized that all the balloons at each table had a different number. So, as the toilet paper brides stood on their numbers facing me, Thomas said, "Please turn to your right." They all turned to the right, "Please turn to your right again," he told them and all their backs were to me. Thomas again gave a command, "To your right ladies," and then his final command came. "Now face Judge Bride." They all looked so serious, they were smiling as if they were trying out for America's Next Top Model. I was too tickled about the whole situation. The paparazzi was still snapping pictures, and flashing every five seconds.

Finally, I started judging. Per the little rule box at the bottom of every sheet, I could only use a number from one through ten once, with ten being the best and one being the worse. So, I figured I would start at number one and work my way up to the best. As I was looking at them indecisively, they were all making different postures and smiling. Each dress kind of looked just like the next except one. It was the toilet paper bride standing on number seven. Not only did they make sure to incorporate the sequins and beads, but they also made a head piece with the toilet paper with sequins on it. Yes, number seven would get the score of ten.

Once I decided who would get ten, I just wrote any number for the rest of the teams. I then gave the score sheets to Thomas, and he looked them over and said, "Congratulations table number seven! You have made the prettiest toilet paper bride dress." Table seven screamed and ran up to the bride, which was one of Mama's friends, and again the paparazzi started snapping. They took one last picture with me, and then Thomas asked them to take their seats.

"Our last and final game is called Twenty-One." Thomas announced. It was a card game. "Whoever gets twenty-one first at each table is the winner. There are special cards inside each deck, and if you end up with both special cards with Edward and Tamara's picture on them, you automatically get twenty-one." He told them that they were to play a total of five games, and whoever won the most games would be the overall winner for that table.

His assistants were passing out the boxes of cards. I was interested in seeing what they looked like, and no sooner than I had that thought, Thomas walked up to me and gave me my own deck. Of course, they were purple and white, and looked like regular playing cards. As I searched through them, I finally came to the one with me on it, and it had a Q in each corner. I kept looking and got to Edward's, and his card had a K on it. Q was worth ten points, and K was worth eleven. Again, I was amazed with Thomas and his staff. I wondered how much my parents paid for this well-organized event.

While they were playing cards, I texted Edward and told him how nice everything was going. He and I texted back in forth for the next five minutes. He asked me how things were going with his mother and me. At that very moment I knew for a fact that Edward knew that his mama was a trip, but I didn't say anything about her being trifling earlier. I just wanted to do all that I could to keep the peace. That's in the Bible somewhere too. I remember Mama reading it one morning to Lamar and me after we had a big argument.

"Time is up ladies, so figure out who your winners are. There is only one winner per table and that person should keep the deck of cards." Thomas had put an end to the last game for the evening. His assistants were once again on point, and began walking out with gift bags. "Will the winner of game two please come to the front? That's all the ladies from table seven. The winners with the deck of cards from each table, please come up front." After Thomas called them all up front, he came over to me and asked if I wanted to present the special gift to Sammi that I had. I told him that I would do it last, she was also the winner of game one.

There was a total of twenty-one winners, and there was a total of twenty-one gifts. After Thomas gave them all their gift bags, and his assistant paparazzi finished snapping shots of me with all of them, they all went to their seats. I then took the microphone from Thomas and asked Sammi and Mama to come to the front. I started to tell everyone thank you for coming, and the serving staff started bringing out the meal.

"I would like to thank each one of you for coming out and celebrating with me. I am so excited about my new life with Edward, and want you all to know that your prayers are much appreciated." Once I was done, I gave Mama the microphone and she said, "First I would like to bless the food," so she said a prayer over the food. "Now I would like to introduce everyone to my other daughter. This is Samantha Daniels, my lovely daughter-in-love, and Tamara and I would like to give her a gift for having Lamar's heart."

Everyone clapped, and Sammi cried a little. I personally was ready to get to that table and eat that food, because it was smelling so good. I gave her a hug, and told her that I loved her. Everyone was eating, and Thomas came back up to say, "This is the last time you will be hearing my voice. Tamara will be opening gifts, because this is her night, but because her heart is so big she has made sure everyone has a gift bag. So, on your way out, you can receive your bag from the check counter. Thank you again for attending, and have a wonderful evening."

The shower went on, I opened gifts, and my friends and family lingered away one by one. I was ready to head home myself. I had a wonderful time. There was staff to put all my gifts in Mama's vehicle, and they also packed up extra food for us to take home. As we were walking out, Mr. Thomas came up and told Mama thank you. Mama said, "Thank you young man. You did a wonderful job, and everything was so efficient." He handed Mama a survey card, and asked her if she would complete it and mail it back in as soon as possible.

CHAPTER TWENTY-FOUR

Too Much Information

I wasn't sure if Mama would be waking up Mr. and Mrs. Wilcox to pray, but why I doubted her I don't know. She woke them up just as if they were her own family sleeping over. I said, "Mama, how do you know these people want to wake up and pray this early?" She looked at me and said, "Because they are in my house, and as for me and my house, we will praise the Lord." She was as serious as anyone could be too. All I could think was, when my husband and I come to visit we're staying at the hotel.

Everyone got up and prayed. Mrs. Wilcox offered to lead prayer, and Mama let her. I was glad that she prayed because I felt like she was apologizing to me for being mean through her prayer, and I forgave her right then for real this time. After prayer, I said, "I'm going back to bed, I don't want any breakfast." Mrs. Wilcox helped Mama cook, and Daddy and Mr. Wilcox went out to the pool.

I must have been tired, because I had missed texts messages, phone calls, and lunch. It was 2:30 p.m. and I was just getting out of the bed. I washed up and went downstairs. When I walked in the den, Mrs. Wilcox was sitting there alone, and Mr. Wilcox was putting their bags into their car. "Hey Mrs. Wilcox, where's my Mama?" She looked as if she was crying, or had been crying. I asked, "Are you okay?" I was praying my mama hadn't gone off on the lady about something.

She pulled herself together and said, "I wish my husband and I had a relationship like your parents. They really don't mind love on each other." I tried to interrupt her because I didn't want to hear this, but then she said, "Mr. Wilcox and I haven't had sex in about four months." Oh, my goodness. Is she having this discussion with me? I wish she was crying because of Mama now. Anything, but this.

Okay, God what should I say? Then my mouth opened. "Mrs. Wilcox, I'm not sure about the situation, but maybe some self-evaluation would help. I know the Bible speaks about a nagging woman causing a man to go to the rooftop. I guess that rooftop could mean anywhere but with that nagging wife. Being kind and loving turns away strife. As long as I can remember, my mama has always been a totally different woman when it comes to my daddy. She's hard, strong, and means what she says when it comes to everyone else. However, when I watch her with Daddy, she's supportive, she lets him lead, and she's very humble. She knows how to allow him to be the head as God has ordained."

I wasn't sure how she was going to take it. I was calling her a nagging wife, but she was telling me about her sex life so, I figured I could go there. She looked at me and said, "You are wise beyond your years. You are going to make

Edward a remarkable wife. Thank you, and I love you." Mr. Wilcox walked in, and Mama and Daddy walked out of their room. I just looked at them with embarrassment all over my face. I couldn't believe these freaks didn't just wait another twenty minutes and let the people leave before they got busy.

Mama said, "Thanks for coming, and drive safe." I gave both Mr. & Mrs. Wilcox a hug and told them I'd see them next week, and thanked them for coming. They all said their good-byes, and I went upstairs so I could call Sammi and tell her about her freaky in-laws. I still couldn't believe Mrs. Wilcox had a conversation with me about the lack of intimacy in her life. That was way too much information for her to share with me. Now every time I see her I'm gone be wondering if she been broke off.

This is another reason I gotta make sure I ain't no nagging wife, because Edward does have his daddy blood in him. I don't want no breaks. I know there is no good reason for a man to cheat, but exactly where does a nagging woman send that man for four months? I'm going to pray for my in-laws, and that Mrs. Wilcox does evaluate herself to find how she can be more loving and win her husband's heart. I just hope she doesn't think that I want to be talking to her about it; it's just too much information for me.

CHAPTER TWENTY-FIVE

So Much Going On

Several days had passed and there was only a week and one day until the wedding. I don't know why I had butterflies in my stomach thinking about it. Edward would be in later today for his bachelor's party, and he was bringing a few of his buddies from Stone Mountain. They are in the wedding, but I had never met them. I don't know how I felt about that. I wasn't stressing it because Lamar was in charge, and Daddy and Mr. Wilcox would be there. Mr. and Mrs. Wilcox were due to arrive back today as well, but they would be staying a whole week this time. They planned their vacation around the wedding.

Sammi said the party was going to be at *Hooters*. I hoped she was right. That's a public place, and that made me believe nothing too crazy would be happening. The next morning, Edward had to leave for his trip to New York, but would be flying back in the same evening for our rehearsal dinner. I was kind of mad about that. The announcement for the rehearsal dinner was out in enough time for him to find someone else to handle this. He did ask me to go, so maybe I will.

The doorbell rang, and I was excited because I thought it was Edward. I ran downstairs looking as glamorous as I could, but it was Mr. and Mrs. Wilcox. Daddy was giving them directions to Dove Resort; it was a very nice resort close to Winterville and Orlando. Since they would be here vacationing, there was no need for them to stay at my parents' house. Mama and Mrs. Wilcox were talking, while Daddy was giving the directions. I heard Mrs. Wilcox talking about Disney World. I loved Disney. I couldn't help but wonder if she had got her some. She seemed relaxed and happy. I wish she had never put these thoughts in my head. I heard Mr. Wilcox say to her, "Come on baby, let's get over there so I can come back tonight for Edward's bachelor party." I thought, "Yeah, they're good now."

As we were walking out, Edward pulled up with his buddies. I started smiling, and making sure my hair was in place. He got out of the car, and I wondered who he would hug first his mother or me. He surprised me, he gave my mama a hug first, then his mama, and then he shook Daddy's hand, and then hugged his daddy. Then he looked at me and said, "I saved the best for last." I'm keeping this man. He keeps me blushing. I said as I was blushing, "Hey babe!" Then he sounded like an old man as he said, "Gimmi some suga." So, I got on my tippy toes and he picked me up and gave me a kiss. I whispered, "I love you, babe," and he echoed me. All his friends were standing there, and he introduced them to our parents. It was four of them, and they all seemed to be nice. I had only spoken to them by phone. They were very handsome black men, and all fit except one that was kind of husky. That's what Mama use to call Lamar because she didn't want to call him fat. She used to tell us that fat was a mean name to call anyone.

Mr. Wilcox said, "Well son, we're headed to the resort, so I'll see you tonight." They got in their car, and left. I wondered if I should have offered to go with them so Mrs. Wilcox wouldn't be alone tonight, and then Mama said, "Tamara, we have so much going on today." I wanted to chill out with Edward, but I knew we had to go pick up my bridal gown, my shoes, all my accessories, and I had to help Mama get the house ready for the dinner after rehearsal and grocery shop.

Mama then let me in on the fact that Mrs. Wilcox would be coming back with Mr. Wilcox to help her get things ready for the dinner. Since the dinner would be at our house, I knew my mama would have me cleaning everything she could see. So, I decided to call my loving sister-in-law over to help me out.

The time went by, and Mama and I had gone to pick up my bridal gown, my shoes, all my accessories, and we went to the grocery store and purchased everything she had on her list. On the way home, Mama stopped by and picked up Sammi from work. I saw Lamar and told him, "You better not have nasty strippers at Edward's party." He started laughing and said, "Girl shut up. We're men of God. We don't get down like that." I could tell that Sammi was flattered that he said that because she was blushing. "Negro please!" Is how I responded.

Mama, Sammi, and I headed to the house, and once we got there we took everything inside. Mama said, "Okay ladies, we will take a lunch and nap break, and then we will get to work about 6:00. I was glad those were the directions, because I was tired. Sammi and I took all my bridal things upstairs to my bedroom, and put them in the closet. We heard Mama yelling from downstairs, "Don't go up there playing dress up!" We laughed, because we use to play dress up in Mama's closet all the time as kids.

I had twin beds in my room. I lied down in my bed that I normally slept in, and Sammi laid in the other. I asked, "So how's the baby doing?" "Fine, we are going to find out the gender September 17th." I told her that I was excited for her. "Sammi, promise me you will let me know as soon as you go into labor so we can come down." She looked at me with such sincerity, and said, "Tamara, your husband travels. You are not going to be able to just up and come to Florida when you want to."

She had a good point. I replied, "But if I want to come and he is working, what's the problem?" She told me to just wait and talk it over with him before I start making plans. Sammi was dozing off to sleep. I picked up my phone, because I decided that I wanted to go with Edward on Saturday to New York. I texted, "Hey babe, can I still go to New York with you in the morning?" He replied immediately, "I already have your ticket." I was happy that he knew me so well. I thought it would be great to have some alone time away from all the crazy wedding stuff.

The more I thought about it, I wasn't sure how nice it would be. We would have to get to the airport by 5:00 a.m., the flight was at 6:00 and was like two and a half hours. He had a meeting 9:00 a.m., we would need to be back to the airport no later than 2:00 p.m. for our returning flight, and then get ready for rehearsal dinner. That was a lot, but I wanted to spend time with my man, so whatever it takes.

I decided to take a nap. Mama would be beating on the door in a few hours to wake me and Sammi so we could get started.

CHAPTER TWENTY-SIX

No Worries

After Mama woke us up, I called Edward to see what he was doing. "Hey babe, what are you up to?" I tried to sound as if I had no worries he was running with his buddies. I wasn't sure what they were getting into. They weren't from around here, and Florida weather tended to make some dress with less material. He told me that they were at the tuxedo shop. I completely forgot that they had to go and take care of that today.

I asked him what I should pack to take to New York. "NOTHING!" I was hoping he meant nothing because we didn't need clothes, but I knew he meant that we would not be there long enough to have to change. "Well you know I'm not going anywhere without at least one change of clothes." I waited to see what he would say after I said that, but he was laughing with his boys about somebody's pants being too short. I hung up the phone, I felt ignored.

The Wilcoxes arrived, and Mama and Mrs. Wilcox got started preparing for tomorrow's dinner. I told Mama I would be back; I was going to take Sammi home. "Sammi, do you think I'm too selfish to ever be a mom?" She said,

"What's wrong now, Tamara?" I explained to her that Edward was just ignoring me on the phone, so I hung up on him. She said as she was yawning, "Child by the time it's time for you to be a mom, you will be tired of being the center of Edward's attention."

"Not real sure how I feel about your statement, but whatever. Get out. Love ya." Before I went back home I stopped by Chic-fil-A to have a little me time. I pulled out my little Bible and decided to just spend some time with God. Reading the Bible was enlightening. I felt God's peace with me as I read His Word. I didn't realize it until I got in the car to go home, but while I spent that time with God I had no worries about Edward's party, no worries about him neglecting me, and no worries about the wedding. God's peace surpassed everything else that was on my mind. Wow!

When I returned to the house, Mama and Mrs. Wilcox were still in the kitchen. Daddy and Mr. Wilcox were sitting in the den watching a Sanford & Son marathon on T.V. "Why aren't they getting ready?" I asked Mama concerning Mr. Wilcox and Daddy. She said they were ready, just waiting on Lamar to come and pick them up. Why? Who needs to be the designated driver? Nobody's drinking. "Tamara, what goes on with the men tonight and their reasoning for doing what they do is none of our business." Mama said with a very solemn look on her face.

I went in the den and sat down by Daddy. "Hey Daddy," and he replied, "Oh boy, what's the matter Baby Girl?" "Nothing, I'm just bored." Daddy looked at his watch and said, "Well it's 6:15 and..." the doorbell rang and interrupted his sentence. It was Lamar; he was always interrupting something. "What's up Big Head?" He said looking at me. He shook Mr. Wilcox hand, and nodded at Daddy. Then he went in the kitchen, "Hey Sexy Mama, you got it smelling good in here." "Hello, Mrs. Wilcox." While he was in the kitchen trying to taste test whatever Mama and Mrs. Wilcox was cooking, Daddy and Mr. Wilcox were getting up, and ready to go.

The doorbell rang again and I just sat there slouched on the sofa watching Sanford & Son. I knew it was Edward, but he hadn't tried to call me since I hung up on him, so I wasn't running to greet him at the door. I grabbed my little Bible out my purse again, I needed that peace I had just thirty minutes ago. How could I be getting all discombobulated already? That taught me a lesson. I must keep the Word of God on my mind, or I'll ease right back into that old me.

"Hey babe," He said when he walked in the room. Daddy and Mr. Wilcox had already walked in the kitchen to tell the wives good-bye. So, I took a deep breath and responded, "Hey babe," and I reached up to give him a hug. He told me he loved me, gave me a big hug, and said he would see me later. I just smiled and watched him walk out. I wondered why he said he would see me later. Why would he see me later? Oh well, I just stayed there and watched the Sanford & Son marathon.

I guess I fell asleep watching the marathon, but it was still on when I woke up. I got up and went into the kitchen. Mama and Mrs. Wilcox were not in there, and it appeared they were done. I walked out to the back porch, and they were sitting back there talking. I didn't go out I just listened to hear what they were talking about. Mama was telling her that she should go to Victoria Secret and pick up something cute to wear at least once a week. I heard Mrs. Wilcox say, "I'm not as small as you are," and Mama told her "It don't matter. Your man will love whatever you put on, as long as he can get it off." That was more than an ear full, so I just went up to my bedroom.

I texted Edward goodnight, and told him I loved him. I wondered how the party was going. I made sure I had everything ready for the morning and I set my alarm for 3:00. I needed to get up and moving so I could be ready when Edward came to pick me up. I wondered what his friends would be doing while we were in New York. I know they had a room at the Hotel Inn, but they didn't know their way around. Oh, well, I'm sure they will figure it out. I went to bed with no worries, just excited about going to New York and making memories with Edward.

CHAPTER TWENTY-SEVEN

Love Is In The Air

My alarm went off, and I hit the snooze button. I laid there another minute or two, and then I got up and went straight to take a cold shower. If I didn't let that cold water hit me I was not going to stay awake. I prayed while I showered, brushed my teeth, and did my hair. I grabbed my bag, and I walked downstairs to the kitchen to get me a banana and some orange juice. I walked pass the den and saw that the sofa bed was pulled out. I looked to see who it was, and it was Edward.

I went in to wake him, and question him about being here. "Good morning handsome. What are you doing here?" He said, "Hey babe." "Oh no, stop talking. Go brush your teeth." His alarm on his phone went off as he was walking to the bathroom to wash up. I made us both a pop tart, an him a glass of orange juice. That's about close as I get to preparing breakfast on my own. When he came back, he asked me if I was ready to leave. I told him yes. I figured I would get the details on the ride to the airport, about him sleeping over.

He grabbed his bag and my bag while I was writing my mama and daddy a see ya later note. We loaded up his car and left. I was very happy to be spending time alone with Edward. I wondered if I would be able to travel with him a lot once I moved to Stone Mountain with him. I had never been on an airplane before either, so this short flight would get me ready for the long flight we would be taking on our honeymoon.

We chatted on the way to the airport for about five minutes, and then I fell asleep. When I woke up we were pulling into the parking garage. I was very surprised Edward didn't ask someone to bring us to the airport so he wouldn't have to leave his vehicle in the parking garage, but I guess it was only for a few hours. We made good time, plus we didn't have any bags to check, so we had time to sit at one of the shops to get a cappuccino.

I asked, "Edward how did your party go last night?" I wasn't sure I wanted to know, but I had already asked now. He told me that they had a great time laughing and talking together, and it was just clean fun. I was happy to hear that. They are men of God, and men of God can have fun without it being naughty. We finished our cappuccino, and we walked to find our gate.

We heard the call for loading and we got in line. I had butterflies in my tummy. I was very nervous about the flight, and Edward knew it. He grabbed my hand and said, "Relax babe, it's going to be fun." How can a flight be fun? We aren't children. What can we do on a flight to make it fun? I was seriously rethinking this whole thing. Why did I have to decide to go? We had plenty of time to be together when he came back. My mind and emotions were going crazy, and I felt like I was having an anxiety attack.

My heart was racing, and my hands were sweating as we stepped onto the plane. We were greeted, and directed to our seats. Everything seemed so close to me. Lord have mercy, we gotta sit this close to people for two and a half hours. We sat down and there was a third seat, and I told Edward that I didn't want to sit by the window because I was scared. I didn't want to sit in the middle because I would have to be that close to a stranger for too long, and I didn't want to sit on the aisle because people would keep passing by me.

Edward looked and me and handed me a pill. "What's this?" I asked, he said, "It's an anti-stress pill. It will calm you down." I asked, "Is this legal?" He looked at me as if I said something to attack him. "Tamara, I love you. Do you think I would give you anything to hurt you?" "Bobby loved Whitney," and I took the pill. I ended up sitting by the window, and pulling down the shade. As I sat there I couldn't understand why it took so long to pull off. I looked around and everyone appeared to be in their seats. The attendant's voice over the speaker started giving directions. She didn't sound very convincing that the plane wouldn't crash. "Why is she telling us all of this? Does she think that maybe we will actually need this stuff?" Edward just kissed me, and it was nice. I know he only did it to shut me up, but it was a very soft kiss.

Finally, the plane started moving. I could feel myself more relaxed. We're off the ground. If I had not of taking the pill, I would have been a total nut case. After about twenty minutes, the attendant came around and offered us drinks. I had water with lemon, and Edward had a cola. I wasn't sure if he still drank or not. We hadn't even discussed that since he gave his life to Christ. I was holding his hand since we took off, and I was finally ready to let it go. Oh my goodness, it felt like the plane hit something!

Edward quickly said, "It's only turbulence," and he kissed me softly again as he put my hand on his face. It seemed as if we kissed for about twenty seconds. I didn't care how long it was it was very nice. He said, "Lift the shade babe, and let's look out together." I thought that was so cute. I opened the shade with my eyes closed, and took a deep breath and then I looked. It was amazing, and I loved that I was sharing it with Edward. I wasn't sure how much more time we had, but I didn't care. My racing heart had turned to a heart of love. Love was certainly in the air.

Once we landed, Edward reached up and got my purse. We got off the airplane, and he asked me "So, how was it?" I told him it was beautiful because he was there. We caught a taxi and I enjoyed the sites. We ended up at a beautiful hotel, and I wondered if we had a room. How perfect would this be? I wondered if Edward was being secretly romantic. "So babe, are we checking in?" I was smiling anticipating his answer. "No, my meeting is here."

The hotel was very pretty. Everything was so tall in New York. I told Edward I was going to look around while he was in his meeting. "Please don't leave the hotel Tamara; New York is big and busy. My meeting won't last too long I promise, and we can go to brunch when I'm done before we go back to the airport." I wanted to see monumental things, however, Edward was right. I wasn't used to such a busy place, and I was kind of tense that he had to leave me alone at all.

It seemed like everyone was rushing. I just walked around the hotel, and took in the sights that I could see from the windows. Once Edward was out of his meeting he called my cell phone. I answered, "Hello." "Where are you at love?" I told him I was riding down the escalator near the conference room he had his meeting in, and as I was approaching the end, he was there to meet me with his beautiful smile.

"How was your meeting babe?" "It was great, and not as long as I thought it would be." It was 10:30 a.m., and I was hungry. He asked me if I wanted to go to Dunkin Donuts, and I looked at him with disappointment. "No dear, I can eat Duncan Donuts back at home. I want to try something that is original for New York." So, believe it or not, we stopped at a food truck. They sold good food out of a truck. I was looking in to see if they had running water to wash their hands, and they did. It was very tasty. There were little iron chairs and tables with umbrellas to sit at. It was romantic to me.

Once we were done, we got in the taxi and headed back to the airport. I was snapping shots of the tall buildings with my cell phone. Edward asked, "Do you need another anti-stress pill?" I told him I didn't think so, but he gave me the bottle of pills to hold in my purse anyway. The flight was okay, because Edward made it okay. Once we got in his car I took the anti-stress pills out my purse and said, "I guess I don't need these anymore." He laughed and said, "Read the bottle Tamara." I read and realized, they were only vitamins. I laughed. We made it back in time for the rehearsal and dinner, and everything was lovely.

Praise God for Edward, and Mama.

CHAPTER TWENTY-EIGHT

Wrapping Things Up

Sunday morning was nice. We all met at Golden Corral for breakfast before church. The entire wedding party was there. I loved spending time with family and close friends. Daddy blessed the food before we rushed off to the buffet line, and Mama said, "Okay we have about an hour until morning service starts, so let's get it in so we can move out." We were all going to Mama and Daddy's church, and she was thrilled about that. It just so happened that they were having Family & Friends service that Sunday. Once we were done, we went to church full and some even looked as if they were nodding during the service. The pastor called Edward and I up at the end of service and prayed for us and our marriage. I thought that was nice.

This was my last week to be a single woman, I had six days until the wedding day. We were wrapping things up daily, but there were so many distractions for us. Edward's friends were here on vacation, his parents were here on vacation, and my friends had taken vacation as well. Thank God that Mama was the drill sergeant that she was, because if it wasn't in her book for me, it wasn't happening. Unless of course Daddy said it was happening.

Tuesday, Mr. and Mrs. Wilcox took Edward and me to Disney. Yey! Mama allowed it to happen without a fuss, so I assumed she knew about it. I didn't care that we were going with his parents, because I was just happy to be going to see Mickey Mouse and ride the It's a Small World ride. Once Edward and his parents arrived to pick me up, I ran downstairs and realized that my parents were going too. It made sense because they had season passes, and Mama loved to eat turkey legs with Daddy as they watched the shows. She could cook those turkey legs herself, but the memories her and Daddy made were magical.

We had a blast at Disney. When we left the park, Edward rode back with Mama, Daddy, and me because his parents were staying over at their resort. We dropped him off at his hotel with his friends, and my parents and I went home. He texted me, "I had a great day with you and the parents." I did too, and I was glad that we had that moment together. I texted him back, "Me too babe, see you in the morning at the church." I hoped he hadn't forgotten that we had marriage counseling in the morning. He texted back, "I know babe, but do we really need it?" I texted back, "Yes," but if the preacher said we shouldn't get married, were we going to call the wedding off?

Edward picked me up the next morning after prayer, and we went to the church for counseling with Pastor James. I had known him since I was a little girl, and Mama picked him to counsel us. He asked us all kinds of questions, showed us different scriptures in the Bible about love, and told us that having an argument was not grounds to not have sex or get a divorce. He talked to us about being faithful to one another, communicating honestly and daily with one another, and most importantly making sure God was the center of our marriage. We both left there feeling blessed, and knowing we were going to do all that we could to make sure our marriage was flourishing.

Later that evening, Sammi and the other ladies in my wedding party threw me a bachelorette party. It wasn't as big as the bridal shower, and only for a select few. It started at 6:00 at the house out on the patio by the pool. It felt more like just a hangout for me and my friends, but Mama and Mrs. Wilcox were in the house bringing out food and drinks. Daddy had left with Mr. Wilcox to get out of the house. My parents and Edward's parents were becoming very close, and I thought that was nice.

Mama walked out and said, "Okay it's time to open your gifts." I didn't see anyone come with gifts, so I looked around. There was a table with three gifts on it. I looked at the tags and they were all from Mama. "Mama why would you buy me anything else, you've done so much already." I opened them and one had a very sexy negligée in it. I was borderline embarrassed that Mama gave it to me and everyone saw it. They all chanted, "Work it girl," and other encouraging words. The next box had matching heels inside. I was okay with that because the shoes were beautiful, and they matched the negligée. The last box was big, and kind of heavy. I didn't know what it could possibly be.

I opened it and it was a pole. Everyone was laughing, and I said "Mama, what am I supposed to do with this?" As soon as I said that the doorbell rang, it was a lady that I didn't know or why she was here. She had a suitcase with her, and Mama introduced her to us. "This is Lizzette, and she is going to show us how to keep toned using a pole like the one I just gave Tamara." Mama must have seen the look on everyone's face because she said, "I'm teaching my baby one way to keep her husband happy at home. Plus, this is good exercise. Don't judge me, I've been happily married longer than all of you have been living," as she pointed at everyone excluding Mrs. Wilcox.

Lord have mercy, my Mama done signed us up for a pole dancing class. If I ever had any doubt what so ever I was now without doubt that my mama was a bonafide, sanctified freak. This was so embarrassing. My friends were clapping, and laughing. Ms. Lizzette was done with teaching us how to pole dance, so she pulled out coin skirts so she could teach us how to belly dance. The belly dancing was fun. I was not surprised that my mama knew how to belly dance and she looked good doing it.

We were all laughing, and it was all clean fun. Mama said, "Ladies, if you have a husband give Lizzette a call and she will teach you some dance moves that you and your husband will love. Don't be trying none of this stuff with no husband, because you end up dancing in hell. That's why I waited three days before Tamara's wedding to give this to her." I knew she wasn't going to let them leave without letting them know that she believed this is for married women, or something like that.

CHAPTER TWENTY-NINE

Wedding Day

Saturday, August 30, 2008 had finally come. Mama walked in the bride's room at the beautiful Victorious Church, and she said, "It's time Baby Girl." Miss Mia did my make-up, Miss. Chanel had just put the finishing touches on my hair, and Mama opened her bag, took out Grandma's pearls, and put them around my neck. "I'm so proud of you baby, and you are going to make a wonderful wife." I kept my eyes closed, because I didn't want to start crying.

I heard the piano start playing "Usher Me," and that was my cue to walk down the aisle. Daddy was standing there waiting for me as I came out of the bride's room. My daddy had tears in his eyes, so I pulled his handkerchief out his pocket from inside his jacket and I dapped his eyes. He kissed my cheek and said, "You will always be my baby girl." Again, I didn't want to cry and ruin my makeup, so I closed my eyes and took a deep breath. I got up on my tippy toes and whispered back to him, "I love you too Daddy."

Daddy tapped the door, and the ushers opened both sides so we could walk in. Everyone stood, and I closed my eyes for what seemed like thirty seconds as I trusted my father to lead me safely down the aisle. When I opened my eyes, we were only a few feet away from the front where Edward would receive me. Everyone was smiling and they all looked so beautiful. The church was absolutely exquisite. Edward walked towards us and the Pastor said, "Who gives this woman to be married to this man?" Mama stood and came to stand with Daddy, and as he released my arm Mama put hers in his, and they both put my hand in Edwards hand and said, "We do." My heart was racing. I was excited and nervous all at the same time. Was this happening? I was about to be Mrs. Edward Wilcox.

I walked with Edward to the altar and we stood in front of the Pastor. Edward looked back at my parents and said "Thank you." The ceremony went on, and finally the pastor said, "By the power vested in me, I now pronounce this man and this woman, husband and wife. You may now kiss your bride." Edward gazed into my eyes and said, "Eternite et un jour" and I said, "Siempre y un dia mi amor." That was how we felt about it, forever and a day. He said it to me in French, and I replied in Spanish. Of course, I added my love to the end of mine.

We walked out and people blew bubbles. We got into a stretch limo, and Mama came up behind us, gave me a kiss and said "The driver has been instructed to take the scenic route getting you to the reception hall, once you get there you can come to the designated area and I'll have clothes and..." I looked at her with widened eyes and yelled, "Mama!" She closed the door as she was saying, "Y'alls married now."

Edward looked at me and I looked at him and said, "Husband." I smiled from ear to ear, but he seemed to have something on his mind. I felt a little perturbed that we hadn't been married for 15 minutes yet and there seemed to be some kind of wall up. I had to ask, "What's wrong babe?" He looked at me with such distress in his eyes and said, "There's something I need to tell you."

NOW! There's something he needs to tell me now? Clearly this is something he could have told me before the wedding. WOW! I was in disbelief, but I kept a smile on my face, I asked "What is it my love?" His voice was kind of shaky like he was uneasy about saying it but he did, "Okay, so I know I put a lot of pressure on you about sex, but I just want you to know that I respect you so much for making me wait. I love you so much for making me prove to you that I loved you enough to wait for you to be my wife. I adore you so much for knowing that your body is the temple of the Holy Spirit." I thought, "Lord is he getting ready to tell me he cheated on me?" I stopped him, "Edward, I know all of this, what's wrong?" The limo driver pulled up to the reception hall. What Edward said to me almost knocked me off my feet.

People were standing outside to welcome us with flower petals and snapping pictures, but my mind was astonished with the information Edward had just given me. Of course, Mama ran and opened the door before the limo driver could. She asked, "Should I close my eyes?" Edward looked at me and said, "Yo mama nasty?" I shook my head and said, "A freak."

"No Mama," Edward and I stepped out of the car and

cheers and applause came from everywhere. The wedding party took pictures, we laughed, and the memorable dances were amazing. Of course, after I changed out of the wedding dress into a more comfortable dress the electric slide took place with my daddy leading the way. The food was tasteful, the toast was heartwarming, and the event wasn't too long. We did not open gifts at the reception; all gifts were put in this beautifully decorated wheelbarrow to be pushed out and loaded in Edward's car as it filled during the reception. After the reception, Edward and I got in his car and went to the Hampton Inn.

The ride there was very quiet; we held hands, but I think we both were thinking about the conversation in the limo. Once we arrived to the hotel, it was kind of extra special because there was a banner that read, "Congratulations on your Union." Complete strangers handed flowers and balloons to us as we entered. Once we arrived to our room, Edward opened the door and picked me up. This was like a fairy tale. The room was beautiful, and I had to be the happiest woman in the world.

Edward had already been to the room and made it romantic. There were flameless candles, white chocolate strawberries, white wine, and 5 roses all different colors. I was too overjoyed to even ask what they meant, but he walked me over to the bed and sat me down and picked them up and said, "Each rose has a special representation to express my adoration for you. Red is because I'll love you forever, pink shows the appreciation I have for you, white is for our new beginning, orange declares the blaze you put in my heart, and yellow depicts the joy I have that you are my wife, my friend, and my lover." This dude is gone get the best that I've got. I could not believe he came up with this all by himself. Then he leaned in and kissed me.

Edward and I met each other on a new level for the first time, as husband and wife the way God ordained it to be. I was worried about not knowing what to do, and come to find out, Edward had saved himself for marriage as well. That was the big news in the limo ride. Edward had talked the talk, but never walked the walk. He put on a front for his boys, like a lot of young people do. I was so happy that I didn't give in; because I didn't give in to my flesh we both were made stronger. I was still hearing Mama in my head saying what she said to me many times, "Baby girl, the flesh is a freak to every born-again believer. Your flesh will always seem odd to your spirit, and your sanctified spirit will always seem odd to your flesh. They will never want the same things. Don't give in to your flesh, and your spirit will produce blessings from God.

Yes, Edward and I did get a little closer, and we enjoyed doing so. Oh, what a blessing from God. This was indeed the happiest day of my life, and we still had forever and a day. We both loved the Lord, and we loved one another. I'm very excited about going to Stone Mountain, and on our honeymoon, too. We could not have done this without God, and of course Mama.

SANCTIFIED FREAK

For the flesh declares what is contrary to the Spirit, and the Spirit, what is contrary to the flesh. They are in conflict with each other, so that you are not able to do whatever you want.
GALATIONS 5:17

BY. SMITH WRITES